AF373933

denied by the alphas

Dawn of the Alphas
Book Three

layla sparks

Copyright © 2024 by Layla Sparks

All rights reserved.

No part of this book may be reproduced in any form or by any electronic or mechanical means, including information storage and retrieval systems, without written permission from the author, except for the use of brief quotations in a book review.

content guide

Thank you so much for downloading *Denied by The Alphas*!

This book has explicit scenes that involve werewolf knotting and omega heat. There is also pregnancy throughout the book.

chapter 1

. . .

Carmen

"I'll call you later," I said quickly into the receiver as I hung up. Harsh knocking sounded on my bedroom door before he barged in, eyes blazing with anger.

Henry, the leader of all packs, wasn't happy about my best friend and her pack escaping the compound. I had to warn her what was happening.

"Where's Ruby?" Henry demanded, his voice low and threatening. His eyes bore into mine, searching for any hint of deception.

"She's on her honeymoon!" I shouted, now fed up with Henry. If he thought he could bully me like other omegas, he was completely wrong. At the same time, I wondered why the hell he was so concerned about her whereabouts.

"Don't lie to me, Carmen," he snapped. "You were just talking to her. This is crucial."

"I'm not lying," I said, breathing hard. I just wanted him out of my apartment so I could have some peace.

Earlier today, he had been questioning me in my living room until I'd had enough. I shouldn't have called her, but I didn't want to give out information that could get her or her pack in trouble. Henry walked into the living room of my tiny apartment, and I followed.

"Do you want some water or something?" I asked flippantly, just to show him he wasn't welcome.

He took deep breaths; his short, angry frame looked almost comical as he stood in my sparsely furnished living room.

He grabbed a sofa pillow and began ripping it to shreds. Feathers flew everywhere.

I stood there frozen. *What the hell was his problem?*

"No, I do not want water," he gritted out.

I stared at him, shocked while he breathed hard, his face red with fury. I didn't even want to question him. At this point, I just wanted him gone. He was like an angry toddler.

"Okay," I said in a low voice.

He dropped the remnants of the pillow and rubbed his face vigorously.

"I don't understand why the packs are leaving the compound," he said. "Am I really such a horrible pack leader?"

"Of course not," I lied, trying to appease him even though I knew he was wrong for not allowing the packs of the compound to be free.

Alphas were free to go wherever they wanted, but they had a set number of days and always needed to report at the checkpoint. On the other hand, omegas like me always needed an alpha to leave the city.

"Then tell me where the Crawford Pack is," he demanded again.

"As I said, they're on their honeymoon," I repeated, terrified but holding my ground because I had no idea where they went.

His alpha scent of tobacco filled the air as he stalked toward me. I tried to move farther away, but my back hit the edge of the kitchen counter. Henry gripped my arm, and I gasped when he became physical.

This alpha was seriously losing his mind.

"Let us both hope you're telling the truth because if I ever find out that you're lying to me," he hissed through gritted teeth.

"I swear I'm not. I don't even know where they went," I said, and something about my final answer seemed to appease him. He released my arm and nodded to his three guards.

Without another word, Henry and his guards left my house through the front door. I stood there for a second in pure shock before finally running over to lock it. I sagged against the door as I tried to take deep breaths to calm myself. I had just been on the phone with clients for my babysitting business before Henry showed up.

This afternoon had turned into a complete nightmare.

As I collapsed onto my squishy couch, I glanced around sadly at the feathers scattered across the floor. My place wasn't great, with wear and tear everywhere. The dirty yellow wallpaper hung from the walls, was dotted with small holes. This apartment was the most affordable option I could find on my own until my business would take off. I tried to process everything that had just happened.

Even if I knew where Ruby went, I would never tell Henry. He was officially out of his mind.

My legs shook once the adrenaline wore off. I managed to walk to my mini work table in the corner of my living room, which was covered in papers.

Glancing at the schedule, I saw that I was assigned to care for an omega and her newborn baby overnight, but I was far too shaken to handle it.

Picking up my phone, I dialed Gracie, one of my beta workers.

"Hey, Gracie," I said hesitantly. "I'm really not feeling up to sitting tonight at Luna's house. Would you mind taking over for me?"

"Of course!" Gracie replied cheerfully. Her passion was babysitting, and I was so happy to have found her to help. "Take care of yourself. Don't worry about it, okay?"

"Thank you so much. You're a lifesaver," I said, breathing a sigh of relief as I hung up the phone. With my evening free, I decided to visit my family, only two blocks away.

It had been a while since I started my babysitting business and even longer since I'd seen my family.

I quickly removed my nose ring in the bathroom mirror, knowing it would only trigger a rant from my mom about how trashy it was. I just wanted to see my siblings, not spend time arguing with her. Dealing with Henry today was exhausting, and it was one of those moments when having a pack of alphas to protect me would have been wonderful.

Unfortunately, I didn't have a pack.

I made sure to lock up after I left since I was living on the sketchier side of town.

***

As I stepped outside, I was glad to get away from my home for a bit. I needed to forget about Henry and his ambush. He was an asshole, and thinking about that helped me avoid crying or breaking down.

I made my way between the closely packed buildings as the sun began to set. The gritty sand crunched beneath my feet with each step, and the air carried a faint scent of sweat and dust. I knew I was getting close to my mother's apartment when I heard Francine's excited shrieks.

My nine-year-old sister was always staring out of the window people watching.

"Carmen!" she squealed, throwing open the door before I could even raise a hand to knock. "You're here!"

"Hey, Franny," I smiled, ruffling her hair affectionately as I stepped inside.

My mom's voice immediately rang out from the depths of the apartment.

"Take off your shoes!" she snapped without looking up from the couch, where she was meticulously applying nail polish. I complied silently, not wanting to upset her. Our relationship had always been tense, and I couldn't remember the last time I'd felt like I'd done something that made her happy.

Her alphas, who were my fathers, had left her years ago for another omega, and it was just us. I was pretty sure that had made my mom bitter over the years, even worse than she usually was.

As I walked into the living room, I was greeted by a giant portrait of Henry. Mom loved our alpha leader for some reason, and his image seemed to cover every available wall space. My stomach churned just thinking about how awful and selfish he was.

"Come," Francine said as she tugged on my hand, leading me towards the small bedroom she shared with Lena, my nineteen-year-old sister. Lena was sitting in front of her vanity, applying makeup with shaky hands. I noticed a small bruise under her eye and frowned in concern.

"Hey, Lena," I said softly, trying not to startle her. "Where are you going tonight?"

"Um, I'm meeting the alpha I've been dating," she replied nervously, avoiding eye contact with me. I instantly wondered what the hell was going on and if she was okay.

"What happened to your eye?" I asked.

"Nothing, I ran into a branch like a dumbass," she said quickly. "Don't worry about it."

"Who's the alpha you're dating?" I persisted. She'd never dated a pack before, and I was officially worried for her now.

"I'll tell you when I'm sure of him."

"Will we ever find out who he is?"

"Maybe," she said evasively, quickly applying foundation over her bruise.

Francine and I exchanged worried glances as I sat on the bottom bunk next to her. My little sister changed the subject, sensing my concern.

"Do you want to see the charm bracelets I got from school?"

"Sure," I answered with a tight smile, but I was worried about Lena the whole time Francine talked on and on.

Later, after spending about an hour with Lena and Francine, I prepared to leave. But as soon as I was about to exit the home, my mom stopped me.

"Carmen," she said. "Have you found yourself a pack yet? Even Lena knows how important it is to be mated."

"No," I said.

"Well, you need to get started," she said disapprovingly. "You're getting older, and you don't want your alphas to get disgusted by you in just a few years."

I rolled my eyes, holding back my tongue. I didn't want to insult the status of her relationship because it was too heartbreaking—even for me.

The night I found out that my three fathers had left, I wasn't sure if it was because Henry commanded them to do it or if they did it on their own. I was ten years old at that time, and I never forgot when my mom explained that I would never be seeing my fathers again.

IT WAS dark by the time I made my way back to my place, a sense of unease settling in my stomach.

Nightfall was never my favorite time, especially with the possibility of alphas lurking around. My scent blockers had been on for nearly eight hours, and I knew they would start to wear off soon.

As I approached my door, I noticed a wolf prowling nearby. His ripped ear was unmistakable—it was my landlord. He'd been hitting on me constantly since I moved in, and tonight was no exception. He shifted into alpha form, and I quickly turned my gaze away from his nakedness.

"Really?" I exclaimed, feeling disgusted. "You think that's going to impress me?"

Tim laughed, his voice dripping with arrogance. "Aw, come on, Carmen. Better get used to this view since you won't be packless forever. I could be your alpha."

"Will you move out of the way?" I said, trying to focus my eyes on his face instead of his small dick.

"Actually, I have to talk to you about something. I saw Henry come by your place," Tim said. "Are you in any trouble with the law or whatnot?"

"What the hell?" I sighed, rolling my eyes. I didn't have the time or the energy for this right now.

"You heard me."

"Well, I'm not in any trouble," I said.

"That's all I needed to know, omega. Have a great evening then," he said with a scowl as he shifted back into wolf form and bounded down the street.

God, he was such a creep.

It was like I had no privacy around here, and I quickly ran into the house and locked the door with shaking hands. I caught a whiff of Henry's lingering scent in the air, and my nose curled in disgust.

Determined to cleanse my home, I grabbed some sage

from the kitchen and lit it, allowing the fragrant smoke to fill the air. I waved the burning sage through each room, focusing on purging Henry's presence from my safe space. Once I finished, I began the tedious task of vacuuming up the feathers strewn about from the shredded pillow and cleaning the rest of my apartment.

It felt like an obsession, but I needed to erase any trace of him. After an hour of cleaning, I finally decided that I was done. Everything was put back the way it was. My orange couch was tucked into its corner, and the non-matching patterned rug was straightened out again. The feathers were all gone, and I decided to take a shower to get rid of all the bad memories.

The hot water was soothing against my skin as I lathered the soap all over me, vigorously washing every inch. Afterward, I crawled into bed, unable to shake the memory of the conversation with my mom about finding a pack to mate with.

There wasn't a pack I wanted to be with, except for the alpha who rejected me four years ago. Suddenly, the memory of his rejection flooded my mind:

It was my eighteenth birthday, and Tyler had promised me a night out while I waited at home for his phone call. He said he would be here at five. I redid my makeup a million times, but he still wasn't here.

Suddenly, I received a call from my friend Jessica.

"Hey Jess," I said.

"I know where he is."

Driven by frustration and confusion, I searched for him, only to find him at a sleazy strip club, hurling dollar bills at half-naked dancers.

"Tyler, what are you doing?" I shouted over the music, tears streaming down my face. "You're supposed to be my mate!"

He laughed cruelly, his eyes cold as ice. "Run along, little omega. Only alphas in here."

"She's clearly not an alpha," I said, glancing at the smiling dancer, who was oblivious to our argument.

"Well…"

"How about us?" I choked out, unable to comprehend his heartlessness.

"There is no us," he said coldly, dismissing me as if I meant nothing.

"You kissed me, though."

"That doesn't mean anything. Haven't you ever kissed anyone before?"

The rejection hurt deeply. My heart ached as tears rolled down my face from his cruelty. Biting my lip, I rushed out of the strip club, never wanting to see his face again.

THE MEMORY of that night still stung, and I hugged my pillow tight, trying to hold back fresh tears.

I really thought Tyler was my destined mate, but he'd shattered that dream with just a few words. Now, even after all these years, it was hard to give my heart to an alpha, and I never wanted to be in that position again.

chapter 2

. . .

Tyler

The wind whipped through the dark forest as we searched for the dead alpha. I shivered as I trudged alongside Axel and Jaxon, my packmates, and also guards, as we scanned the ground for any signs of Marrok, Henry's son.

We had been tasked with finding him, and the pressure was mounting.

"Do you think Marrok got lost chasing squirrels or something?" said Axel.

"Or maybe he's off stalking some unsuspecting human," Jaxon added, chuckling.

I gritted my teeth, anxious about the possibility of not finding Marrok and having to tell Henry the bad news. "This isn't the time for jokes. We have a job to do."

As we neared Marrok's cabin, I spotted claw marks in the dirt.

"Look here," I said, pointing them out. "Two wolves, by the look of it. It's no surprise Marrok had enemies, and kidnapping an omega didn't exactly endear him to others. Let's follow these tracks and see where they lead."

"Right," Axel agreed. "I wouldn't be surprised if we found him dead."

"Wish he was," Jaxon replied.

We tracked the wolf footprints a short distance from the cabin. Marrok didn't get too far before he was taken down because I suddenly saw a shallow grave hidden among the trees.

My heart thundered in my chest as Axel dug up the muddy earth with a shovel, revealing a gruesome sight—a wolf's head buried beneath leaves and twigs. The killers hadn't even bothered to bury it properly.

"Marrok," I whispered, picking up the severed head by its matted hair. The features were shrunken and twisted in death, but I recognized him all too well. A wave of relief washed over me; as much as I hated to admit it, the world was better off without someone as corrupt and dangerous as Marrok.

Still, this would only serve to push Henry into a frenzy. I pulled out my phone and dialed his number.

"Yes, Tyler. How's the search going?" Henry answered.

"Henry, I've found your son. He's dead," I said simply. There was no sugarcoating it; there was no proper way to say it.

"Dead?" Henry asked softly, his anger palpable. "The packs are getting out of control, and I *will* find them."

"How would you find out which pack is responsible?"

"I know exactly which pack is responsible and the omega who's in cahoots with them. What was her name? Ah, Carmen," he said, and my blood ran cold at the familiar name of the omega I rejected years ago and never talked to after.

"I'm sure she has no idea what happened here," I said coolly, trying to distract him before he could focus on her.

"Yes, that may be the case, but I'm not a stupid wolf."

"Are you going to have a funeral for Marrok?"

"Funeral? No, we'll have a celebration instead. They

would never attend Marrok's funeral, but the wolves love to party. We need all the packs to attend so I can lay down some new rules," he snarled. "Now bring Marrok's head to someone who can examine it and find out who did this."

As I hung up the phone, my stomach churned with conflicting emotions. My loyalty to Henry warred with my growing hatred for him—a man who cared more about power than the well-being of his own son. But my job was to ensure the safety of the packs, nothing more. With disgust, I placed Marrok's head into a black bag and prepared to return to the Alpha Compound.

THE SUN STARTED TO SET, casting an eerie glow over the road as we drove back to the Alpha Compound. My phone buzzed relentlessly in the cupholder, my mother's name flashing on the screen each time.

"What is it this time?" asked Axel as he eyed my phone.

"She really wants us to find an omega and produce grand-kids for her," I said, ignoring the phone as I drove.

"Well, we're eagerly waiting, too," Jaxon said with a smirk.

I sighed and glanced at the screen, feeling a mixture of guilt and annoyance. I knew that if I went too long without visiting her, she'd think I hated her. But I was tired, and after today, I just wanted some peace.

"Besides," Axel added, "we're constantly busy working for Henry. She should understand that. Wasn't it her idea for you to become a guard in the first place?"

"Actually, it was my fathers who pushed me," I corrected him, knowing that all that mattered to my family was being close to Henry and gaining the prestige that came with it.

I didn't want to let them down after they insisted I apply

for the job as Henry's security. My fathers were all successful in the community of wolves, and my mother made sure to only associate herself with other high-ranking omegas in our society.

As I drove, I worried about Henry's focus on Carmen lately. Now that Marrok was dead and Henry was unstable, she was in jeopardy, and I needed to check on her over the next few days.

We pulled into the driveway of our spacious home. The house had enough room for our entire pack, and all the alphas had their own space which was good, or else we'd drive each other nuts.

I groaned when I saw my mother's car parked out front.

"Looks like she's here since you won't visit her," Jaxon laughed as we climbed out of the car.

"Great," I muttered, plastering a smile on my face before entering the house. My mother stood in the kitchen, meticulously applying icing to a cake.

"Hello, son," she said in a high-pitched tone, which meant she was excited about something. She was a short omega who wore fur coats and designer shoes to prove that she was better than the other omegas.

"What's the occasion?" I asked, trying to sound casual, but I instantly knew she had ulterior motives.

"Tyler," she beamed. "I've found the perfect omega for you! High status, from a reputable family, and absolutely beautiful."

My smile faltered, and my face hardened. "I'm not interested right now, Mom."

"Oh, really? And why is that?" she asked, already getting upset as she crossed her arms over her coat.

"We're not ready, and my pack also has to have a say in who they're going to mate with for the rest of their lives."

The truth was that any omega I brought home would be

within reach of Henry. Working so closely with him meant that starting a life with an omega would be a disaster.

Henry could easily decide to steal an omega or reassign her to another pack.

My mother sighed dramatically, adjusting her luxurious fur coat—a symbol of wealth that she wore with pride. She always demanded that I marry a high-ranking omega, someone who could elevate our family's already prestigious position. But she wasn't giving up just yet.

"Tyler, this omega is perfect for you. When are you going to be ready?"

"Who knows?" Jaxon interjected. "Maybe when we accidentally get one pregnant."

"He doesn't mean that, ma'am," Axel said respectfully.

Her gaze narrowed, and she left the house in a huff. Looking at the white cake, I shook my head. I didn't like disappointing my family in the slightest, but I needed to set boundaries.

Once she was gone, Jaxon flopped onto the couch. "So, when are we really going to find ourselves an omega? I'm tired of temporary flings."

"One day, it'll happen," I assured him. "We just need to be patient. Maybe after we leave Henry's task force."

"That's impossible," Axel said. "We signed up for life."

My heart sank at his words, and I suddenly remembered the night I rejected Carmen. As much as it hurt at the time, I knew it had been the best thing I could do for her.

chapter 3

. . .

Carmen

Two days later, the moon cast a soft glow through the nursery window as I gently rocked the sleeping baby in my arms while his new mother slept in the next room.

His tiny breaths were warm against my chest, and I couldn't help but feel a pang of longing deep within me. I loved helping new omega mothers through the night, providing them with much-needed rest while caring for their precious little ones. As I thought about my tasks ahead—washing bottles and preparing the next round of milk for the baby—I realized just how much I craved having a pack and a baby of my own.

"Maybe it's time to move on," I whispered to myself. Lately, I had been remembering Tyler's rejection, which still haunted me. I knew I shouldn't dwell on it because he wasn't my fated mate after all, but the memory still hurt.

As I placed the baby in his crib, I watched as his tiny fingers curled around his blanket. Making sure he stayed asleep, I quietly tiptoed out of the room and into the kitchen. I stood at the sink, letting the warm water run over my hands as I washed the baby bottles, lost in my thoughts about how I was going to find a pack. Maybe I'd have my mom help out, but the idea of talking to her made me anxious.

With all my tasks done for the night, I decided to call it a night. I yawned as I gathered my water bottle and snacks into my backpack before heading out.

As I walked home, I tightened my jacket against the chilly wind.

The narrow streets were lined with small houses constructed close together to keep the compound tightly knit. Occasionally, I spotted an alpha guard in wolf form patrolling the area. I didn't worry about them—it was the alphas without uniforms I had to watch out for, the ones who harassed omegas like me.

My heart dropped when I saw Henry standing at my front door, a paper in his hand.

What the hell was he doing here?

My pulse quickened as Tyler, the alpha who had rejected me years ago, emerged from the shadows behind him. Our eyes met, and heat flushed my face, my body responding to his presence.

"Umm, hi, Henry," I greeted, trying to sound polite even though fear clawed at my insides. Three a.m. was never a good time for a visit unless it meant something terrible had happened.

"Hello, Carmen," he said slowly.

The anticipation of what he was going to say next built within me, making me feel nervous. But that was Henry; he liked to play games.

"Is something wrong?" I asked.

"Many things are," said Henry. "But lucky for you, I'm here to personally invite you to the party I'm hosting this Saturday."

Oh wow. My family and I were never invited to these sorts

of parties. Only the elite were invited, and my mom would throw a fit if she knew I was asked and she wasn't.

He handed me a card, and I looked at it, pretending to read it, but my brain was a jumble this late at night.

"Thank you, I guess, for inviting me. I have work though, and..."

"Nonsense," he said. "Isn't it your own business that you're running?"

"How do you know...?"

"I know everything about you, Carmen," he said, and I could see Tyler's eyes flashing in the background. "It would make me really happy to see you there."

I nodded wordlessly, my mouth dry.

He was acting like my presence at the party would be monumental for him. I couldn't fathom why he'd be interested in a poor omega like me. Then, just like that, he walked toward his waiting car. Tyler turned back one last time, his gaze lingering on me a moment longer before he followed Henry.

Quickly unlocking my door, I bolted inside and vowed never to leave my home again.

I COULDN'T SLEEP that night; my thoughts were still racing from the invitation and the fact that Tyler was working with Henry. I knew some loyalists would die for Henry, but others disagreed with him. My emotions were all over the place, so I decided to call my alpha friend Logan, even though it was three in the morning.

"Are you *insane*? It's three a.m.," Logan groaned when he answered the phone.

"Logan, listen," I pleaded, my voice shaking. "Henry came

to my door tonight. He personally invited me to a party at his house this Saturday."

"Wait, what?" His tone changed instantly from annoyance to alarm. "Are you sure?"

"Yes! Why would I lie about that?" I said, anxiety making me short-tempered. "He showed up with Tyler, of all people."

"Shit," Logan muttered. "This isn't good, Carmen. If Henry went through all that trouble, he might be thinking about making you his omega."

Dread rose within me at the realization. *How could I be so dumb?* Henry replaced his omegas all the time.

"Can you come to the party with me? Bring your pack if you want and any omega that you're dating," I said, desperate for any kind of protection from whatever Henry had planned.

"Fuck, Carmen, I can't just take time off from painting," Logan sighed, clearly hesitant. "And no, I'm not dating anyone."

"Please, I need to show him that I have a pack," I begged, on the verge of tears.

"Alright, alright," he relented. "I'll be there."

"Thank you," I whispered before hanging up. The image of Henry's predatory gaze haunted me as I tried to fall asleep, shaken and uneasy.

THE FOLLOWING DAY, I was jolted awake by a loud knocking on my door. Panic set in as I wondered if Henry had come to claim and mark me. Padding softly to the living room, my fear mounting with every step, I peeked through the peephole. My eyebrows furrowed in confusion as I saw Tyler standing outside.

"Shit," I mumbled, racing to the kitchen to wash my face. I tied my messy hair into a ponytail with a scrunchie and glanced down at my polka-dotted pajama set. Tyler would probably think I was so immature when he saw my clothes. But who the hell cared what he thought anymore?

Flinging the door open, my heart pounded in my chest when I saw Tyler. He even looked taken aback for a moment.

"What do you want?" I snapped rudely, noticing his two packmates standing beside him. Their faces were unfamiliar; I'd never met them before.

"Can we come in?" Tyler asked, his voice serious. "We need to talk."

"Sure," I replied with a hard edge. They filed into my apartment, and I couldn't help but feel the tension in the air. I wondered what could possibly have brought Tyler here. "Why are you here?"

"Don't go to the party," he finally said, his expression grave.

I laughed, momentarily forgetting my nerves. "Why are you trying to control me now? I'm all grown up, you know."

"Yes, I can see that," he said, his gaze darkening as his eyes settled on my chest. "But it's not that. I know Henry, and he's dangerous for you."

A pit formed in my stomach, knowing that he was right. But I wasn't prepared to admit that to him.

"I'm going to go if I feel like it," I said, crossing my arms over my chest, my face burning. "I don't need your permission, and I don't want to get on Henry's bad side."

Tyler's jaw tensed as he looked at me. "My packmates Axel and Jaxon will be checking in on you often. Just to make sure you're safe."

"Safe from what?" My breath hitched, and I could feel the heat pooling between my legs as Tyler stared at me intently. "Why do you even care?"

He didn't answer, instead getting up from the couch

silently. *Jerk*, I thought bitterly. *Why would he care if I was Henry's omega or not? He threw me away like I was nothing.*

"Hey there, I'm Axel," one of the strangers said, holding out his hand. He was muscular, with short-cropped blond hair and warm blue eyes. His smile was welcoming, and I found myself smiling back despite my grumpiness as we shook hands. "Nice to meet you, Carmen."

"Jaxon," the other alpha, covered in tattoos, introduced himself, his eyes lingering on my lips. Jaxon was pretty good-looking, and it made my heart flutter just looking at his floppy brown hair covering one eye.

"Just to reiterate—I don't need any protection," I announced to the pack at large. "Especially since I'll be looking for a pack to mate with soon."

At that, Tyler stopped in his tracks by the door, his back stiffening. He didn't say anything, though, and continued on his way out.

"Bye then!" I shouted after him, slamming the door behind them.

***

Tyler

AS I WALKED AWAY from Carmen's apartment, I was at a loss for words.

Seeing her so grown up and sexy, dressed in those loose, flowing pajamas with her hair framing her face, had left me breathless. My cock was hard as I remembered the scent of her —a scent I knew all too well. Her scent was like fresh limes, invigorating and intoxicating, and it had an undeniable effect on me.

"Damn, Carmen is hot as fuck," Axel commented, breaking me out of my thoughts.

"She is," Jaxon chimed in. "Did you notice how much stronger her scent got the longer we were there? She definitely felt something, too."

"Do you think she's open to us being her pack?"

"Enough," I growled, cutting their conversation short. "We're not mating her. Our only priority is making sure Henry doesn't put his knot in her."

The thought of that happening made my blood boil, and I vowed silently to myself that I would never let it occur. I'd protect Carmen, even if she didn't want me to.

chapter 4

. . .

Carmen

Saturday arrived, and I was a nervous wreck as I sat in my living room, taking deep breaths to calm the panic rising in my chest.

I really didn't want to go to Henry's party, but I was all ready and waiting for Logan to pick me up so I didn't end up going alone.

My black formal dress clung to my figure, the high slit up the side revealing a hint of my thighs. It was the plainest dress I owned, but I still felt uncomfortable that it might draw attention to me. I finished the look with simple black pumps and wore my hair loose around my shoulders after blow-drying.

As I waited for Logan and his pack to pick me up, I couldn't help but wonder—what if I were Henry's next omega?

The thought terrified me.

I wouldn't know what to do if Henry had his sights on me. Even if I tried to escape, he was powerful and wealthy. He would find me.

Looking at the clock, my heart started racing as it got closer to the time Logan agreed to meet me. I didn't regret asking him to accompany me; I needed a couple of strong alphas by my side to pretend I had a pack.

A knock on the door startled me, and I nearly tripped over my heels as I rushed to answer it.

Standing there, a smirk on his face, was Logan. He looked pretty good in a tailored suit that accentuated his lean, muscular frame. His wavy black hair was styled casually, giving him a dangerously attractive appeal.

"Can't believe I'm going to this party from hell with you," he said darkly, giving me a huge hug. "But I missed you, lady."

"You're so amazing for doing this," I replied, hugging him tightly and feeling that warm connection I always had with him.

Griffin and Talon stood behind Logan, his packmates.

"Long time," greeted Griffin, pulling me into a giant hug that nearly engulfed me.

"Hey, Grif," I said, smiling. His hugs always gave me comfort during my down moments. He was a stout alpha of shorter stature with a toned body. His silvery-grey eyes seemed to look into my soul every time we talked, and his warm chocolate scent calmed me.

"Hey, babe," said Talon, who always seemed to be flirting with me even though I wasn't their omega. His midnight-black hair and sharp green eyes, along with his vanilla scent, created a dangerous combination for any omega. I couldn't help the clenching between my legs as I hugged him next. "You look stunning."

"I'm trying not to be," I said quickly. "I don't want Henry getting the wrong idea."

"What's wrong with him?" he teased with a glimmer in his eye.

"He's in his sixties," I replied, rolling my eyes. "I'm not going to mess with him."

"So what's the goal here?" asked Griffin, crossing his arms and looking ready for war.

"I just want to make an appearance and leave," I said. "I just need to say hi to Henry, and then we can leave after hanging out for a little bit."

"Sounds good," said Griffin.

"We're already a couple of hours late," said Logan, glancing at his fancy watch. As a punctual alpha, he hated wasting time. I knew he'd rather be at home painting his masterpieces than babysitting me at a party. "Let's go."

DREAD WASHED over me the moment we arrived at Henry's home. It was essentially a mansion that towered over us. I had seen it once or twice but had never been inside.

Anxiety enveloped me as we walked between the imposing wrought-iron gates, guarded by stern-faced security personnel dressed in sleek black suits, adding to the air of exclusivity surrounding the event. Elegant guests milled about on the manicured lawn, their laughter and clinking glasses creating a tantalizing backdrop as we approached the entrance.

"Wow," I breathed, linking my arm through Logan's for support. "I've always wondered what it was like inside these parties."

As we stepped into the lavish ballroom, I couldn't help but gawk at the opulence around us.

The room was bathed in warm, golden light that glinted off the polished marble floor and crystal chandeliers above. Alphas and omegas spun gracefully around the dance floor to the lilting strains of a waltz, while beta servants, dressed in crisp white shirts and black vests, circulated with trays of sparkling champagne flutes.

"This is actually a big deal," Logan said. Griffin stood

protectively at my other side while Talon trailed closely behind us.

The perfume of the omegas was overwhelming as they danced with their partners. Combined with the scent of alpha testosterone, it was making my head spin.

Amid the swirling crowd, I suddenly caught Tyler's gaze from across the room. He looked utterly captivating in his dark suit, and the intensity of his stare made my stomach clench. My cheeks flushed hot with desire, and I tried to ignore the pull I felt towards him.

"Logan," I said, nervously fidgeting with my dress. "I don't think I even needed to come here. Henry probably won't even notice I'm here."

"Well, it's too late now that you dragged me here," he replied smoothly, taking my hands. "Now, how about a dance to take your mind off things?"

"Uh, sure," I agreed, still trying to shake the feeling of Tyler's eyes on me.

Logan led me onto the dance floor, and his hands on my waist stirred feelings within me. My breathing grew harsher at such close proximity, and I started to wonder what was happening. He had always been just a friend to me, but with him practically hugging me, it was becoming something more.

We danced to the music, spinning in circles like the other packs around us. One omega was dancing with three of her alphas at the same time, which looked too complicated for me. I looked up, unconsciously turning my face toward Tyler, and saw him standing there with a hand on his gun, glaring at me.

What the hell was his problem?

"I need to use the bathroom," I blurted out as the song ended, my cheeks burning from our close proximity.

"Want me to come with you?" he asked, a hint of concern in his voice.

"No, it's okay," I replied quickly, not wanting to admit

that I was too flustered by his touch and Tyler's unending glare.

———

As I LEFT the crowded ballroom for some air, I found myself wandering down an opulent hallway. Suddenly, I noticed a room covered in glass, filled with a large number of people.

Walking toward it, I realized what was happening. There was a massive glass wall, and behind it was an orgy taking place on the other side.

Alphas, omegas, and betas were completely naked in this dark corner of the mansion. There were even alphas in their wolf forms, licking and nuzzling the females while an omega moaned in ecstasy, her body filled by five alphas simultaneously.

My face grew even hotter as I took in the scene, my arousal mounting at the raw display of desire before me.

"Would you like to join them?" a deep voice whispered in my ear, making me jump. Henry stood there, smiling at the crowd of indecency on the other side of the glass.

"What the...?" I stammered, flinching away from him.

"Would you like to try it?" he purred, stepping closer. "You won't know until you experience it for yourself."

"No," I managed to choke out in my shock. I could hear my pulse pounding in my ears as I noticed the feral intensity in his gaze.

"You must be a little curious?" said Henry.

"She's not interested," barked Tyler, who suddenly appeared beside us, his strong hand closing around mine. His eyes were intense, and his jaw was tense as he challenged Henry. "Carmen, I'm ready for that dance you promised me."

Henry sighed dramatically, pulling on his regal gold robe.

"Always the cock block, Tyler. Can't you see she's intrigued by my offer?"

"Let her decide what she wants," Tyler replied, never breaking eye contact with Henry.

Even though I hated Tyler to the core of my being, I needed to escape the look in Henry's eyes that would entrap me in eternal misery.

"I'd rather go with Tyler," I whispered, my voice barely audible over the pounding music.

With that, Tyler quickly led me away from Henry, our fingers still intertwined. I noticed Henry's guards following us with their eyes, watching our every move.

My heart raced at the thought of Henry cornering me like that. He had made his intentions clear; he wanted me to be part of his omega harem.

"Thanks for the save," I said in a low voice so only Tyler could hear. I was too shaken up to even care that he was holding my hand.

"No worries," Tyler murmured into my ear. "His guards are watching."

His large hand enveloped mine, warmth radiating through our joined fingers. The touch sent shivers down my spine and brought a flush to my cheeks. I couldn't help but feel drawn to him, even after everything that had transpired between us.

As we approached the dance floor, Logan looked at us in confusion.

His dark eyebrows arched in surprise when he saw me with Tyler, clearly not expecting this turn of events. I gave him a fleeting glance, knowing full well that he would have plenty to say about me dancing with the very alpha who had rejected me.

Tyler pulled me close, his hips grinding against mine as we moved in time with the sultry beat. The heat of his body and the intoxicating scent of him made it impossible to shut off my feelings for him, despite the hurt and bitterness that still lingered.

I tried to maintain a serious expression, but with every touch, I felt weak against this alpha.

"It's been a while, huh?" Tyler said softly, trying to break the ice between us. I remained silent, unwilling to give him the satisfaction of a response. His lips thinned at my coldness, but he continued to dance with me, his hands roaming over my body in a way that made it hard to breathe.

"Why are you pretending everything's fine between us?" I asked, my voice a little shaky from the stimulation of scents and Tyler's hands all over my dress.

"Can I at least explain myself?" he asked, stopping the dance and looking me in the eyes. I could hardly breathe as I gazed back, spellbound.

"Carmen," interrupted Logan, suddenly appearing beside me. I breathed a sigh of relief when he whisked me away from the dance floor and away from Tyler's probing gaze.

"I want to leave," I told Logan, my voice shaking. He nodded without question, understanding the urgency in my eyes.

I walked between Talon and Logan, with Griffin trailing us. We moved quickly out of the double doors and into the night air.

"How the hell did you end up with Tyler?" asked Logan, his voice harsh.

"Whoa, why are you being so weird about it?" I said, surprised by his reaction. He rubbed his face in frustration.

"Sorry, Carmen, but why? I'm just curious."

"Look, I saw something, and I ran into Tyler by accident," I explained, my voice barely above a whisper. "He was trying to protect me from Henry."

"What did you see?" asked Logan.

"Henry has a separate room in his home where he hosts...

orgies," I said, my cheeks flaming. Griffin and Talon chuckled at my expression and the matter-of-fact way I said it.

"He does that," said Griffin.

"How do you know?" I asked.

"Everyone knows—well, at least the alphas do."

As we neared the car, a shout rang out in the night, making us all freeze in our tracks. We turned to see Henry approaching, a displeased expression on his face.

"Why are you leaving so early, Carmen?" he demanded, his voice dripping with false concern. "I was looking forward to spending more time with you."

"I don't feel well," I lied, my heart pounding in my chest. "The party was amazing though, and I had an amazing time."

"What a shame," Henry replied, his eyes narrowing. "But I insist you come visit me tomorrow. I would love to talk more."

"What time?"

"How about noon?" he asked.

"Sure," I replied, swallowing hard and realizing I had little choice but to agree.

"Excellent," he said, lifting my hand to kiss it. His lips on my skin made me shudder, but I hid it well. He felt so slimy to me. "I can smell your fear, omega. Don't be frightened of me."

I nodded, even though his words did little to ease my discomfort around him. He looked satisfied with my nonverbal response and finally turned to leave.

"Oh wow," muttered Griffin, wide-eyed.

"He wants her," said Talon, shaking his head as my stomach churned.

"We'll talk in the car," barked Logan. He seemed upset that he couldn't do much to protect me, especially since he hadn't declared me as his omega.

If he did, we would be bonded for life, but we were just friends.

As we climbed into the car, I couldn't shake the feeling of

dread settling in my stomach. *How had I gotten myself into this mess?*

Logan glanced over at me, his voice low and serious. "He just won't give up, huh?"

"How the hell can I get out of this?" I asked, my voice laced with desperation. "I can't stay here, and I don't want to be one of his... playthings."

"First, you have to see him tomorrow," Logan said, his eyes dark and determined. "But after that, we'll do whatever it takes to get you out of this compound, even if it means leaving everything behind."

I nodded, feeling a twinge of sadness at the thought of leaving it all behind. But I didn't want to lose my freedom, even though it wasn't much as an omega living in an alpha compound.

chapter 5

. . .

Tyler

My pack and I were spying on the omega.

We watched Carmen through the window of her home—her apron clinging to her curves as she chopped onions on a cutting board.

I couldn't help but stare at the way her ass jiggled when she moved around the kitchen. It was hard not to admire her, even though I knew I had to keep my distance. The aroma of the food she was preparing wafted through the air, making my stomach growl audibly.

"You hungry, man?" said Jaxon.

"It smells fucking good," I said, unable to shake off the memory of us dancing together earlier. Holding her in my arms wasn't something I imagined would happen again, but it did.

"She's fucking beautiful," Jaxon said. "Why aren't we making her our omega again?"

"Tyler, why are we here?" Axel asked, breaking my reverie.

"She's the omega I rejected years ago," I admitted reluctantly. My pack didn't know about my past with her.

Jaxon's eyes widened in shock. "Why the hell would you do that? There's nothing fucking wrong with her."

"It was for her own protection," I explained. "I was going to be a guard for Henry, and he would have taken any omega I claimed."

"But that's a risk every pack takes. That's not good enough," Axel said, shaking his head.

"Are you regretting it now?" Jaxon questioned, his gaze still fixated on Carmen.

"We're going to pretend to court her," I told them. "It's the only way to keep her safe from Henry. We'll officially announce it tomorrow when she goes to meet him."

"So we're here to tell her this? That we're going to be her fake pack?" Axel asked. "When we could have been her *real* pack?"

"It's too late to fix the past," I said. "But I can protect her now."

I walked around the house toward the front door and paused before ringing the doorbell. The more time I spent around her, the more I wanted to hold her.

To kiss her. To *knot* her.

But it couldn't happen.

I rang the doorbell, and after a couple of seconds, Carmen opened the door, her eyes widening at the sight of me. Before she could slam the door shut, I jammed my boot between the door and the threshold.

"What do you want, Tyler?" she snapped, clearly not happy to see me, her breasts heaving through the apron with how hard she was breathing.

"I have an idea you might want to hear," I said slowly.

"What idea?"

"It's an idea to keep you safe from Henry," I said simply, and she finally relented, allowing us into her home. As the door closed behind us, Carmen rushed back into the kitchen.

"I hope I didn't burn the onions," she cried out as she stirred the pot furiously.

My eyes were glued to her ass, jiggling beneath her apron as she continued to stir the red sauce. Tearing my gaze away, I started taking deep breaths to calm my erection, which was waiting to burst through and knot this omega.

Leaning against the counter, I watched her, my heart pounding in my chest. As she looked up at me, her cheeks flushed pink when our eyes locked, but there was something in her gaze—like a guilty look I couldn't shake off.

"Are you hiding something?" I asked, unable to shake the feeling that she was keeping a secret from me.

"No," she replied, her voice defensive. "Why would you think that?"

"Just...a feeling," I muttered, though I couldn't help but wonder what she was hiding. I wasn't imagining things, and I knew her even though it had been years.

"Tyler, why are you here?" Carmen asked, her voice guarded as she stirred the pot on the stove.

"Well," I began, trying to keep my tone calm, "like I said, I have an idea to keep you safe."

Carmen's eyes narrowed. "What kind of idea?"

"Maybe we could pretend to court you so that Henry sees you have a pack interested in you."

She turned her head away sharply, focusing on adding layers of cheese to the casserole-type dish she was making. There were tears in her eyes, and my chest ached, not knowing how much pain my past rejection had caused her.

"I'm not interested in your idea. It's too painful, and I don't like that," she finally whispered.

I nodded, understanding the toll my rejection had taken on her. Swallowing hard, I asked, "Why haven't you mated with a pack yet?"

"None of your concern," she retorted, and I silently agreed. "Are you hungry?"

"No, I'm fine," I replied, even though my stomach growled slightly.

"Hell yeah, I'm hungry," said Axel, and I glared at him, annoyed. I wanted to leave immediately after my proposal, but now we would need to stay for dinner.

"Food will be ready soon," Carmen said with a smile at Axel.

Carmen

I WANTED nothing more than for Tyler and his pack to leave my home. Since my tiny house didn't have a dining table, they ate in the living room. The house was quiet for a bit as they dug into their food. I sat on a single chair across from them, a plate in hand. The casserole tasted good but a little salty. I wondered if the pack noticed.

"Carmen, this food is amazing," said Jaxon as he slurped up a giant bite.

"Thanks," I said. "I'm glad it's not too salty for you."

"Oh no, it's great," said Axel.

My mind drifted to the upcoming meeting with Henry, and I grew increasingly nervous. Tyler caught my preoccupied expression.

"What are you thinking about?" he asked. He seemed to know instantly when something was wrong, but I couldn't tell him that I was leaving this alpha compound forever.

"Henry wants to see me tomorrow," I said, giving him half the truth so he would back off.

"I'm coming with you," Tyler said.

"Fine," I said, knowing this would be the last time I would

see him or his pack. It didn't matter to me either way, since Logan promised to help smuggle me out of here as soon as possible.

"We can help you with the dishes since you cooked all the food," said Axel, and Jaxon nodded. Jaxon took my empty plate, and they started to tidy up the kitchen after I had made a huge mess while cooking dinner.

"Oh wow, thank you," I said, watching how quickly they were moving. I decided to take a break and text Logan not to show up tomorrow morning since Tyler was going to go with me to Henry's.

I quickly typed out a message for Logan while in my bedroom, but just as I hit send, a sudden presence at the door caught my attention. I turned to see Tyler, his piercing green eyes filled with longing. My heart pounded in my chest, the pain of our past mingling with the magnetic pull between us.

We moved toward each other slowly, drawn together as the sound of dishes rattled in the kitchen.

Our gazes locked, and the air around us crackled with desire.

We were inches apart, our lips about to meet, when he pulled away abruptly, causing a sharp sting of rejection to pierce through me once more.

"We're leaving now," Tyler said in a serious tone. "I'll be here tomorrow morning."

"Okay," I replied, hating how my voice squeaked with vulnerability. He turned, leaving me feeling aroused and my heart racing.

I sank to the carpeted floor, exhaustion washing over me.

My body still burned with desire from being so close to Tyler. My pussy throbbed, and I was a quivering mess as I lifted my skirt as soon as I heard the front door slam closed.

I couldn't help it as I started touching myself to relieve

some of the ache that he arose. It had been awhile since I felt these feelings.

I moaned softly as I circled my pussy with two fingers, the sensation sending shivers down my spine. My pussy clenched, slick coating my fingers as my pleasure built. I closed my eyes, wanting to drown in pleasure and relax.

"Need some help with that?" Jaxon's voice interrupted. My eyes flew open, and I screamed as I closed my legs, mortified that he had seen my pussy.

"I thought you all had left," I gasped, blushing furiously. I couldn't believe he had witnessed that.

"I was just finishing up the dishes. But if you'd like, I could finish you off too... with my mouth." His words sent a jolt of arousal through me.

"Y-your mouth?" I stuttered, my heart pounding so hard it felt as though it might burst from my chest.

"Yep. I just need a taste." He ran his fingers along my knees, the warmth of his touch seeping through the thin fabric of my skirt. I wanted his hands to travel under my skirt, but I was too scared to say it.

"Why?"

"Because I've been smelling you all day. Your arousal makes us all aroused," he explained.

"Oh, *moons*."

"Are you a virgin?" he asked, his hazel eyes intent on mine.

"Yes," I whispered softly, and he smiled.

"So, may I taste?"

"Yes," I said, in the mood and not willing to throw him out just yet until he made himself useful.

As soon as I gave my answer, Jaxon lifted my skirt to reveal my exposed, quivering pussy beneath. I couldn't believe I was allowing this to happen, but I was aching for his touch.

If someone had told me that I'd be sitting here with an

alpha's head between my thighs, I would have called them insane.

"Relax, sweetheart," Jaxon murmured, pressing gentle kisses on my inner thighs. His lips felt warm and soft, sending shivers up my spine. I moaned in delight as he chuckled lowly. "You're so responsive. I love it."

I had never been eaten out by anyone before, and the anticipation was almost unbearable.

As Jaxon's mouth trailed upward to my pussy, he planted soft kisses all around it, his breath hot against my sensitive skin. The wet sounds of his lips connecting with my flesh made my cheeks flush with heat.

"Your pussy is so pretty, little omega," he praised, making me blush even more. His words only spurred slick to drip from my core, and he noticed. "Mmm, look at you dripping on the rug."

He began licking my pussy, teasing my entrance with the tip of his tongue before moving up to suck my clit. I gasped and moaned, gripping the carpet as pleasure coursed through me. His tongue swirled around my clit, sucking gently yet firmly, and I could feel the pressure building within me.

"Good girl, open up for me," Jaxon encouraged as I allowed my legs to fall open wider. His praise sent a warm glow through my chest, and I bit my lip, trying to hold back another moan. I felt vulnerable, basking in the attention he was giving me. My fingers dug into the carpet, and my back was flush against the bed as I sat on the floor.

My heart pounded when he wrapped his large hands around my ankles, holding my legs wide open for him.

He looked up at me, his hazel eyes filled with hunger as he continued to suck the slick from my pussy. His tongue swirled around my clit faster and faster, and I knew I wouldn't be able to hold back much longer.

"Jaxon, oh god... please don't stop," I panted, my entire

body trembling with need. The sensation of his mouth on me was indescribable, an all-consuming fire that threatened to burn me alive.

"I need to drink. Come for me, baby," he urged, his voice muffled by my drenched folds. "I want to taste you."

With one final, intense suck on my clit, I shattered.

My orgasm took over, leaving me breathless and shuddering. Jaxon didn't let up, greedily lapping at my juices as I rode out my climax.

"Oh my god," I groaned when he finally lifted his head with a wicked grin.

"Well, that was delicious," Jaxon said, licking his lips, his eyes intense as he gazed at my face. I quickly scrambled to pull my skirt down as he watched.

"That's not happening again," I said, getting up and pointing at the door. "You better not tell a soul about this."

"Do you really think they won't smell you off me?" he asked with a wink. Then he strolled casually out the door before I could stop him.

chapter 6

· · ·

Carmen

The next morning, fifteen minutes before my meeting with Henry, I was sitting in the backseat of Tyler's sleek car.

Up front, Tyler and Axel were discussing something related to their guard jobs while Jaxon sat next to me. His presence was nerve-wracking. I couldn't easily forget what happened last night and the way he ate me out, but I tried to act as normal as possible.

A part of me wondered if he told Tyler and Axel what happened.

"Listen, Carmen," Tyler glanced back at me through the rearview mirror. "I'm going to tell Henry that I'm courting you when we get there. It might give us some leverage and protect you from him."

"What if he doesn't care?" I asked, my voice shaky.

"Then we'll deal with that possibility when it comes," Tyler replied, his eyes meeting mine briefly before returning to the road.

Jaxon's knee brushed against mine, and the forbidden contact sent butterflies through my belly. I bit my lip, staring out the window, pretending not to notice how close he was to me.

He leaned in closer, his lips brushing my ear as he whispered, "You look incredible today, by the way."

I could feel my face heating up, and I tried to take deep breaths to calm myself down. The nervousness of meeting Henry, mixed with Jaxon's flirtatious behavior, was making it impossible to think straight.

Glancing down, I suddenly realized that my simple white dress was see-through. I groaned in horror as I noticed the outline of my thighs and white underwear clearly visible. Henry wouldn't be able to contain himself, even though I aimed for a very simple look today. I didn't even put on makeup.

It would be a recipe for disaster.

"What's wrong?" Axel asked, a look of concern on his face.

"Her dress," Jaxon chuckled, his gaze lingering on my thighs. "A wardrobe error. But I love it."

"Is it really that bad?" Tyler asked.

"It is," I groaned. "You can see my underwear!"

As I stewed in shame, the car suddenly swerved, and I saw Tyler driving toward a mall.

"It's too late for that," I cried out.

"No, it's not. He can wait; go ahead and pick another outfit," Tyler said in a gruff voice, parking right in front of the mall doors. For a brief moment, I was touched that Tyler actually cared.

As I got out of the car, Jaxon hurried out after me, giving me his sweater to cover myself. I quickly tied it around my waist for coverage as I thanked him.

"No problem, beautiful," Jaxon said, taking my hand as we quickly walked inside the mall. "Are you ever going to tell me why Tyler rejected you? Did you piss him off?"

I rolled my eyes. "I didn't do a damn thing. I thought we

were fated mates, and I followed him to a strip club years ago with my friends. Then he rejected me. That's all there is to it."

"Damn, that's all?"

"Yeah," I said as we walked past shops. "I have no idea why he did it, but there must have been a reason."

"He was wrong to reject you," Jaxon said firmly, and heat rose in my cheeks. Hearing that validation from his packmate made me feel a tiny bit better about the whole situation.

We entered a store and rifled through the clothes, eventually settling on a pair of jeans, a shirt, and a black leather jacket. As we waited in line to buy the items, Jaxon grinned.

"Why are you smiling?" I asked, wondering if the colors I picked out were horrible. It was a basic outfit that I would wear to Henry's.

"That's a good choice of clothes. Your dress makes me want to fucking knot you."

"Reign it in, Jaxon," I warned playfully, but my heart raced at the thought. "It's never happening."

"Is that a challenge?" he asked, smirking.

"Maybe," I replied, feeling myself getting aroused, even though I knew he was the wrong alpha for me, and I needed to avoid getting involved with him.

AFTER PURCHASING THE OUTFIT, I rushed to find a fitting room, ripping off the tags. I was only wearing my underwear, and my heart raced when Jaxon slipped into the room behind me, his warmth enveloping me as I tried to focus on getting dressed.

The intimacy of the small fitting room seemed to amplify every sensation, from the heat radiating off Jaxon's body to the faint scent of his arousal.

I gasped as his lips found the nape of my neck, his strong

hands gripping my ass and pulling me closer to him. Every rational thought in my head screamed that this was wrong, but my body betrayed me as he cupped my breasts in his hands.

"God, Carmen," Jaxon murmured against my skin, his voice husky with desire. "I can't get enough of you."

I couldn't get enough of him either.

I could hardly breathe as he moved his hands down my thighs, squeezing them gently before sliding one hand up to cup my center. The feeling of his fingers pressing against my pussy sent a jolt of pleasure through me, making my legs tremble.

He began to massage my clit with his thumb, and the sensation was so intense that I could barely speak. The pad of his thumb was rough against my delicate flesh.

"We shouldn't be doing this," I whispered, even though I didn't want him to stop.

"Doesn't it feel right, though?" he asked, his fingers continuing their relentless assault on my pussy. "I know it's wrong, but I can't help myself. I'm drawn to you."

"Me too," I admitted, unable to deny the connection between us any longer. My eyes fluttered closed as Jaxon rubbed my clit faster, sending me spiraling toward the edge of ecstasy.

Being with Jaxon was hot. And it was *electric.*

"Imagine how good it would feel if I slid inside you right now," he growled into my ear, heightening my arousal even further. "Wouldn't you like it if I took your virginity?"

I couldn't respond as I clung to his muscular arms. My pussy clenched as slick seeped down my thighs, and my legs shook uncontrollably from my powerful orgasm. It felt as if every nerve ending in my body had been set alight, and I struggled to catch my breath.

"Oh my god."

I could feel his thick hard cock pulsing against my lower

back, and all I wanted was for him to be inside me right now. Fucking me on the fitting room floor like no tomorrow and then knotting me fully.

"Better get dressed, sweetheart," Jaxon whispered. "You don't want to be late for your appointment."

His words jolted me back to reality, and I reluctantly pushed him away so I could start getting dressed. My entire body shook as I pulled on my jeans. I would have to shower after I met with Henry, but I didn't have time now. It was already past twelve, and I needed to hurry.

TWENTY MINUTES LATER, I was walking between Tyler and Axel as we headed toward Henry's mansion, with Jaxon following close behind. On our way here, Tyler seemed to know what had happened between me and Jaxon because he appeared quiet and upset. His anger was palpable, and he was short with Jaxon.

To me, it was no big deal, and it had nothing to do with Tyler. So, I chose to ignore him as we walked into the mansion.

"She has an appointment with Henry," Tyler said to two of the guards, who nodded, likely because they knew him. Tyler mentioned that he was the head of security while he was driving, and I felt much safer, even though that meant he worked closely with Henry.

"Hello, darling," Henry greeted me when I entered the dining room. He was wearing a lavish red bathrobe, leaning back in his chair as he sipped tea. Then he turned to Tyler with a scowl. "Why are you here, Tyler? Aren't you supposed to be working?"

"I'm courting Carmen to be the omega for my pack," Tyler replied, his voice steady despite the tension in the room.

Henry's eyes flashed with irritation. "I invited Carmen, not you. You have no right to be here."

"Actually," Tyler countered, "as her alpha, I have every right to be here."

"Then where is your claiming mark on her?" Henry challenged, his gaze focused on my neck. "Would you like to do that now? If you're serious, Tyler, I suggest you mark her immediately."

The room fell silent as my heart pounded in anticipation.

My heart raced as I turned to face Tyler, hoping that this time he would stand up for me and claim me as his own. But his expression was cold, void of any emotion, as he slowly approached me. A part of me clung to the hope that he would finally show some sign of love or affection.

He leaned down to my collarbone, and my heart raced.

Okay, wait, was he seriously going to mark me?! Was I even ready to be mated to him for life?

But suddenly, he pulled away, and it felt like someone punched me in the gut.

A wave of hot tears stung my eyes as the truth crashed down on me like a ton of bricks. He didn't hate me. He felt nothing for me at all.

In this moment, I knew—I knew that he would never claim me as his own, but a part of me hoped that he cared enough to save me.

"Actually," Tyler said, turning to face Henry with a steely expression, "I'm not ready for that. You can have her."

Henry laughed at Tyler's words, and I felt like a pawn in a world of heartless alphas.

As Tyler walked out of the dining room with his pack, I knew my heart would never fully recover from his blatant rejection. I would never forgive him; he had literally delivered me straight to hell, ensuring I couldn't escape.

A servant pulled out a chair for me, and I sat down because I literally couldn't stand any longer.

"Drink some tea with me, beautiful omega," said Henry, as a second servant rushed to serve tea. All I could think about was how easily Tyler had handed me over to Henry without a second thought.

"Your mother is doing well, I hope?" Henry asked, attempting small talk as I forced myself to sip the tea. I wondered what had happened between Tyler and me—what made him hate me so much that he couldn't even bear to claim me as his own.

"Uh, yeah, she's good," I replied, my voice shaky. "She has posters of you all over her house." The thought crossed my mind that maybe he could just have my mom instead; she would be over the moon with that arrangement if she could have Henry to herself.

"Oh, does she?" he chuckled. "You are gorgeous, Carmen. Do you know that?"

His eyes appraised my body, and my cheeks flushed as I took another sip of my tea, trying to mask my discomfort.

"Thank you," I said, still preoccupied with thoughts of Tyler. My chest ached, and I felt shaky, just like the last time he rejected me, but it wasn't as bad.

"Would you like a massage?" he asked suddenly, catching me off guard. I shook my head, but he continued, "Perhaps I'll get one."

He rose from his chair and extended a hand toward me, inviting me to join him. Reluctantly, I took his soft, pillow-like hand, disgusted by his touch, as we walked to the massage room.

As soon as we entered, I wasn't prepared for Henry to drop his bathrobe. His pale body was exposed, and he smirked when I glanced at his erection.

"What the hell?" I muttered, immediately turning away.

I tried to focus on a spot on the wall as the beta female masseuse began working on him. I refused to let him see how affected I was by his presence or that I was shocked.

The longer I stood there, the angrier I became.

Henry's groans filled the room, and I clenched my fists, wanting nothing more than to leave. Eventually, his snores echoed through the space. It was time for me to go, and I quickly made my way out.

As I left the house, I spotted Tyler and his pack waiting outside for me.

"Was it that bad?" Tyler asked, noticing my expression.

"Do you really care about that? What if he knotted me?" I yelled at Tyler, who remained expressionless.

"He doesn't do that on the first day with omegas," he replied. "I work with him. I know this."

"I have nothing else to say to you, Tyler," I said, walking past him and ignoring his car. I just wanted to go home and never see him again.

Jaxon followed me, leaving Tyler and Axel behind.

"Tyler's an asshole," Jaxon said gruffly, trying to comfort me. "I'm sorry, Carmen."

"Leave me alone, Jaxon," I whispered, tears filling my eyes. "I don't want to see you anymore."

He looked as if I had punched him in the gut, but he nodded slowly. "I understand," he said quietly. "We shouldn't have left you."

I continued walking, realizing that I had no one to rely on. I needed to get away from this place and away from Tyler.

chapter 7

Carmen

The scent of freshly brewed coffee filled the small kitchen as I paced back and forth, nervously nibbling on my lip. My co-workers, Gracie and Kaela, sat at the table, their fingers wrapped around warm mugs as they exchanged concerned glances.

"Listen," I told them, pausing to look at both of them. I had just informed them that I was quitting for a short while. "If things get too overwhelming with babysitting, don't hesitate to stop taking clients, okay?"

Kaela shook her head, her curly hair bouncing. "No way. We'll keep Tiny Paws up and running. Don't worry about us."

"Well, I won't be gone for long," I said, sighing heavily. "So, how long do you think I should stay away? Until Henry forgets me or... dies?"

Gracie grimaced. "Honestly, Carmen, I've heard horror stories from omegas who were temporarily in Henry's pack. They get treated poorly afterward because they're seen as *used*. You either need to find a pack to mark you or..."

"I know," I groaned, my stomach churning with nervousness. "That's exactly why I need to leave. Finding a new pack is impossible. I don't come from a prestigious family with money, and no one wants a rejected omega."

"Then what's your plan?" Kaela asked as she poured sugar into her cup. Even though it was ten p.m., they needed coffee for the nighttime shift.

"Logan's going to help me escape," I admitted.

"Oh wow, isn't he like your best friend? What if he makes a move on you?"

"He wouldn't," I said, laughing, but then worry set in the more I thought about it. "Anyways, call me if anything comes up with the business. Gracie, you'll be in charge for now."

Gracie's eyes sparkled with pride, and she nodded. "You got it, Carmen."

AN HOUR LATER, after saying our goodbyes, I retreated to my room and started packing.

As I threw clothes into a suitcase, I wondered if leaving was really the right choice. My heart raced, fear and uncertainty gnawing at me. I glanced at the clock—just one hour before Logan would arrive. I hurriedly showered and dressed in a cozy sweater and leggings.

The doorbell rang, and I licked my lips as I opened the door, ready to get the hell out of this compound. I greeted them at the door with my three suitcases all ready to go.

"Hey, Logan," I said in a quiet voice as if Henry's henchmen were lurking around my apartment.

"Is this it?" asked Logan as he stepped inside to grab a couple of suitcases while Talon took the third.

"Yes," I said. "We should move faster. What if they see us?"

"Don't be worried, Carmen. We're just going on vacation

with our omega fiancée. Nothing to feel guilty about, right, love?"

My heart flipped at his words.

"Right... my alpha fiancée," I said, swallowing.

"It's the only way we'll get out of here," he whispered in my ear, his hot breath brushing against my skin. My heart raced at how good he smelled, like sandalwood mixed with citrus.

"Okay then, if it's the only way," I replied.

"Excellent," he said, suddenly producing a ring from his pocket. I smiled at the effort he put into this. He knelt before me, and my heart was pounding. "After many years of friendship and getting to know you, I've finally come to my senses. Will you marry me, Carmen?"

"Oh, stop," I laughed, trying to ease the mood as I extended my hand. "Oh my god, yes, I'll marry you."

"Good omega," he said, his eyes darkening as he stood back up. In that moment, it seemed like he wanted to kiss me, and my stomach somersaulted at the thought of whether he felt the same tension.

"Okay, cool," I said, licking my dry lips as I turned to lock the front door behind us.

"Let's do this," Logan said confidently while Griffin and Talon effortlessly loaded my suitcases into the trunk. My heart swelled with gratitude for this pack that was willing to help me escape, putting their own lives on the line. As I climbed into the back of the shiny black van, it shook from the weight of the alphas joining me.

"Where are we going?" I asked, biting my lip.

"It's a small town a little ways from here. We're going to Borger," Logan replied. "Seven hours away. You'll be safe there."

I nodded, my heart pounding as I researched the city on

my phone while they started driving. Apparently, it snowed more there than anywhere else in the state.

Suddenly, the van slowed down, and I realized we'd reached a checkpoint. Gripping Griffin's hand tightly, my heartbeat quickened even more as Logan spoke to the guard.

"We're just heading out on holiday with our omega fiancée," Logan explained smoothly.

"What's her name?" the guard asked.

"Carmen."

"Carmen, please step out of the vehicle," said the guard, and my heart thumped uncontrollably. Security had tightened ever since Ruby escaped with her pack.

"Don't worry," whispered Griffin as I reached for the door handle. "If they don't let you go, I'll snatch you up, and we'll get the hell out of here."

Taking a deep breath, I stepped out of the van as two guards inspected my face. They even took note of the ring on my finger. I felt grateful that Logan had thought of it, even though I thought it silly at the time.

"You're free to go. Have a good vacation," the guard said gruffly as I hurried back inside to join Griffin in the backseat.

Griffin pulled me in the rest of the way and slammed the door behind me. "Fuck them all."

"It's okay," I said, giggling at how passionate he was about the entire situation.

"They're getting too controlling," Logan said in a serious tone once we drove past the checkpoint. "They have no idea how many alphas they're pissing off. Henry's lost my support a million percent."

I released the breath I didn't know I was holding and let go of Griffin's hand.

"Sorry," I said to Griffin, hoping I didn't make it awkward between us.

"Don't apologize," Griffin murmured, his eyes soft and his

dark stubble visible in the moonlight. "I wish I could hold your hand the whole time, you know. I enjoyed it."

My cheeks flushed. "Maybe I can just... lay on your lap instead? I'm exhausted."

"Of course you can," said Griffin, his smile widening.

As I rested my head on his lap, he gently stroked my hair.

"Enjoy it while it lasts," said Talon from up front.

"You're just fuckin' jealous," growled Griffin, and I closed my eyes with a small smile. I wondered how my new life was going to be, even though I was scared shitless. I never thought I'd be leaving the only home I've ever known.

***

Tyler

"Isn't it creepy that we're just following her around like this?" my packmate Jaxon muttered as we trailed the van carrying Carmen and the pack she was with.

I clenched my jaw, my grip on the steering wheel tightening.

"I need to make sure she's safe," I replied, my voice tense.

"Safe from what? She's with Logan and his pack," Jaxon scoffed. "They're not going to hurt her the way you fucking did, Tyler."

I fell silent. He was correct.

"I just need to make sure..." I said. "In case they abuse her once they're alone or worse. We have laws on the Alpha Compound, and it's my job to..."

"That's bullshit, and you know it," said Axel bitterly. "Now Logan will make his move on her, and it'll be too fucking late."

"We never had a chance," I said, breathing hard as I swerved to avoid a car and keep them in sight.

A heavy silence fell over the car as I struggled to keep my emotions in check.

Deep down, I knew I should let Carmen go completely. But I couldn't—not while she was still packless and vulnerable.

I wanted to make sure she wouldn't get hoodwinked by some alpha and end up hurt.

***

Carmen

I WOKE WITH A START, feeling something hard poking against my ear.

Blinking groggily, I looked up to find a snoring Griffin beside me. His dark hair fell across his handsome face as he slept, his strong arms crossed over his chest. And I realized with horror that he'd had an erection the whole ride.

Sitting up, my body felt sore as I looked around since the van had come to a stop in front of a home covered in light snow. Oh wow, it looked magical.

As I glanced out the window, I saw Logan and Talon unloading suitcases from the trunk. Griffin stirred beside me, rubbing his eyes before shooting me a sleepy smile.

"Good morning," he murmured, his voice rough from sleep.

"Morning," I replied, feeling my cheeks heat up at the memory of waking up with his morning wood in my face. "It looks like we're here."

"Oh fuck, that was fast," said Griffin, just as surprised as me when he saw the snow.

We both got out of the van to join Logan and Talon, who were pulling the suitcases across the driveway. Griffin grabbed a couple of suitcases, and I was confused as to why there were so many.

Did they really mean to live with me?

"Hey, Logan," I said, unsure how to bring this up without sounding mean. My breathing quickened when he looked my way, and his face brightened with a smile.

"Carmen, did you sleep well?"

"I did," I replied, shivering from the cold. Logan seemed unfazed by the snow and wind whipping around us. "Thanks for driving all this way. I bet you're tired."

"It wasn't too bad since Talon also drove," Logan said, his eyes locked on mine. "Listen, Carmen, we're going to stay here with you for a few days. We want to make sure you're acclimated before we leave."

My heart raced as I stared at him, the wind tousling my hair around and chilling my lips.

"For a few days?" I asked, my voice barely audible over the howling wind.

"Yes, or more if it comes to that," Logan replied, watching me closely. "Let's go inside. You're getting cold."

***

WE STEPPED INTO THE HOUSE, and I was amazed that Logan had secured this place at the last minute. The high ceilings and open floor plan made it feel even more spacious. Logan had really outdone himself, and I smiled despite my life turning upside down.

"Wow, Logan," I said. "I love this place. But seriously, let me pay for my half. I'm not your omega or anything, so it's only fair."

"Absolutely not," he replied, grinning when he saw me checking out the tall windows in the living room and the immaculate kitchen.

"We're not at the Alpha Compound anymore, though," I said playfully as I opened all the cabinets in the kitchen.

"It's still an alpha's responsibility to take care of his... the omega."

I blushed, knowing what he was about to say.

"Well, I won't fight you on it," I said, heading up the stairs to pick out my room. I didn't really care which room I was in, to be honest, as long as it had a bed because I was exhausted.

"I put your suitcases in there," Talon said, nodding toward the biggest bedroom in the house.

"Okay, thank you," I said, and as he left, I couldn't help but think how nice it would be to have an alpha pack of my own. Too bad I didn't have one.

After unpacking my things, I took a shower, letting the warm water wash away my lingering anxiety. I stood in the shower, soaking in this new atmosphere. I had never stayed overnight in a house full of alphas who were suitable to be my mates.

I was about to collapse into the very comfortable-looking bed when I caught the delicious scent of food wafting from downstairs.

My stomach suddenly growled, so I hurriedly unpacked my suitcase while my body was wrapped only in a towel. There was a knock on the door.

"Yes?" I called out, rummaging through my clothes. I needed a pair of underwear—something simple to wear to dinner—but I'd done a poor job of packing.

"We got dinner going," Griffin said. "Came up here to let you know it's time to eat."

"I'm coming," I called back. "I just..."

Suddenly, my towel unraveled just as Griffin had already opened the door, and I jumped as I pulled the towel up to cover my exposed breasts.

"Oh, sorry," he said, standing there as my face heated with embarrassment.

"Griffin!" I yelled, and he hastily turned to leave, his face turning pink. I wondered what he had seen. I sat there on the floor, breathing hard and trying to gather my bearings. I couldn't afford to be flustered around these alphas all the time.

I was an omega who owned a business, for God's sake.

"THE FOOD SMELLS DELICIOUS," I said as I entered the kitchen, my stomach rumbling in anticipation. Talon stood at the stove, stirring a sizzling pan filled with seasoned meat and colorful veggies. Griffin wasn't in the house, and Logan was fiddling with the TV cables in the living room.

"Ah, just in time," Talon said, flashing me a smile. He seemed to be in a good mood. "Want to try some?"

He held up a forkful of the juicy, tender-looking meat, and I couldn't resist.

"Sure," I replied with a hungry grin.

As I reached for the bite, Talon lifted it higher, causing me to lean closer to him, our bodies nearly touching. For some reason, I was hyper-sensitive to this, and he chuckled darkly as if he knew the effect he had on me.

He finally lowered the fork. I took a bite, and my eyes rolled back in delight at the tangy flavors.

"Wow, this is so good," I panted, feeling breathless from our closeness. The heat radiating off his body, combined with the hardness of his cock pressing against me, made my core clench with desire.

"It is," he murmured.

"Aren't you going to move?" I asked, trying to sound casual despite my racing heart.

"Doesn't it feel good?" he whispered, his emerald green

eyes locking onto mine. I could see the lust burning within them, and it was hard not to get lost in his gaze.

"Uh, guys? What's for dinner?" Griffin's voice interrupted our intimate moment, and Talon reluctantly pulled away from me.

"Steak stir-fry," Talon replied smoothly, as if nothing had happened. But the lingering heat between us suggested otherwise. My face burned the entire time during dinner, replaying over and over in my mind how close I had gotten to Talon. As I enjoyed the delicious meal, I envisioned him sinking himself into me thoroughly, exactly the way I wanted.

"What are you thinking about?" asked Logan, noticing my distant gaze and vague answers. I snapped back to reality, my heart racing from the thought of Talon knotting me.

"Nothing at all," I said, even though I was blushing pretty badly, and the entire dining room smelled like lime.

"Tell us," insisted Griffin while Talon looked at me like he was ready to devour me. And man, I wouldn't mind it at all.

"It's not that interesting," I said, my face hot.

"Why are you blushing?"

"Oh, it's nothing," I said, trying to play it off. "I can't wait to go to bed tonight. Aren't you all tired too?"

<hr>

LATER THAT NIGHT- WRAPPED in a cozy cocoon of blankets, I was lost in the world of my romance novel. My heart raced as I read an intensely erotic scene, my breath coming in short, shallow gasps. The room felt warmer than usual, and I could sense the heat rising in my cheeks and slick between my thighs starting to pool.

There was a soft knock on the door.

"Come in," I sighed, about to finger myself.

As Logan entered the room, I looked up from my book,

still catching my breath from the descriptive passages. I clenched my thighs to mask my rising scent of arousal, but it was impossible.

"Wow, what on earth are you reading?" Logan asked with a scowl, his nose twitching as he detected my arousal in the air. The pupils of his eyes darkened with feral energy.

I quickly tried to close the book, but he was faster, crossing the room with the agility and speed of a panther. He snatched the book from my hands, flipping it open to the page I had been reading.

My face flushed crimson as he silently read the passage where two alphas were knotting an omega at the same time. He sighed and set the book down on the bedside table, meeting my gaze with a mix of amusement and intensity.

"Don't read this stuff anymore," he warned, placing the book on the dresser.

"Why?" I replied almost defensively. "Listen, you're not my alpha..."

"Do you want me to rut you?" he asked, inhaling my scent deeply while closing his eyes. "Because if I did, you would be mine. For life."

"No," I said in a low whisper. "But that doesn't mean I have to stop doing what I enjoy."

Suddenly, Logan turned serious. "I came here with a proposal to make."

"Oh?" I asked, sitting up in bed, instantly nervous.

"We've had an amazing friendship all these years," he said slowly, his eyes searching mine. A pang of fear coursed through me as I wondered where this conversation was heading.

"Logan, what—" I started to ask, but he continued, cutting me off.

"Please, let me finish," he said, taking a deep breath. "For years, I've had feelings for you. I've watched you grow into the amazing omega you are today. After everything we've been through, I can't keep this to myself any longer. Do you think I could ever be a suitable alpha for you?"

I was shocked, my mind racing as I struggled to find words.

My heart pounded in my chest, and my breath hitched under the weight of his confession. The ring he had given me sat on the dresser, sparkling under the dim lights, suddenly seeming to hold more value than I had first thought.

chapter 8

. . .

Carmen

$\mathcal{M}$y mouth was dry as I tried to find an answer. I didn't want to ruin our friendship, and I was scared to move on from my past rejection.

"Logan," I said slowly, trying to be as gentle as possible. "I appreciate your offer to be my alpha, but I really don't want to ruin our friendship if we take it there."

"A relationship built on friendship is always a beautiful thing," he said, his brows furrowed as he studied me. "Is it Tyler holding you back?"

My throat tightened at the mention of Tyler's name, but I had to make things clear once and for all.

"No, it has nothing to do with him," I said quickly. "I love the friendship we have, that's all. There's nothing wrong with you or anything."

"Be honest with yourself. Are you just waiting for Tyler to claim you?"

"No, I'm not waiting on him. Not in a million years," I said, sighing under the pressure Logan was applying. My breaths were coming harder, and the room suddenly felt stiflingly warm. I slipped out from under the blankets and pulled on a jacket. "I need some fresh air. I'm going for a walk outside."

"Snow's coming down pretty hard right now," Logan warned. "It might not be the best time."

"I'll be fine," I insisted, zipping up my jacket. Then I quickly put on mittens and a hat. "I'll just walk down the block and come right back, I promise. I just need to clear my mind and figure things out."

"I'm sorry if I made things awkward or anything," Logan said quickly as he followed me out of the room. He sounded sincere, and I looked up at him as my heart ached. There was longing in his gaze—a longing I couldn't fill.

"Don't worry," I said, taking his hand and squeezing it once I was at the front door. His hand felt gigantic and warm, but I needed a moment alone.

He opened the door. "Don't be long. Are you sure you don't want me to walk with you?"

"Yes," I said. "My life has literally turned upside down, and I need to figure it out."

"Alright," he sighed, looking at the pelting snow outside. "I'm coming out there if you're not back in ten minutes."

As I stepped outside, the snowflakes transformed into icy pellets, hitting my skin with stinging force as I walked down the driveway and onto the sidewalk.

My mind raced with thoughts of Logan's offer and the implications of having him as my alpha. I couldn't comprehend the mere idea of him knotting me—his massive member throbbing and expanding inside of me. The pros were that if we did get together, it would be a good thing, and I'd have all the protection I needed. But at the same time, I was scared just in case Tyler was supposed to be my mate. The difference between Tyler and Logan was how I felt around each of them. Tyler evoked those feelings in me instantly since high school—

the butterflies each time he touched my hand or looked at me, the feeling of being weak in the knees.

Looking around, I soon realized I had walked much farther from home than I intended.

The snow was falling steadily, and the silence around me felt almost oppressive, broken only by the crunch of my boots.

All the houses suddenly looked the same.

Oh shit.

Panic rose in my chest as I searched my pocket for my phone, only to groan in frustration when I found it missing. Oh my god, I left it at the house.

No, it's okay. *I'll just find my way back*, I comforted myself.

My teeth chattered as I shivered in the cold, my lips growing dry and cracked. I continued walking, desperate to find my way back, but it felt like I was walking in circles, seeing the same types of houses.

Was I really going to die out here?

I had to find the house no matter what, or else I was screwed. I thought about my family. My sisters would care if I went missing, and Logan would probably care, too.

The blizzard intensified, obscuring my vision until all I could see were snow flurries swirling around me.

My boots sank into the deepening snow, and the flakes clung to my eyelashes, making it even harder to see. I fought the exhaustion creeping over me, trying to stay awake. To my horror, the snow came up above my knees now.

My body was getting tired.

I needed to climb up a driveway and knock on anyone's door. Suddenly, my trembling legs gave out from exhaustion as I collapsed onto the snow just to rest for a little while.

Tyler

WHERE WAS CARMEN?

My binoculars were sitting on the dashboard of my security van after I observed Carmen and her platonic alpha friend talking at the door.

And then, for some reason, he let her walk out alone. *What the fuck was that about?* I thought she went to get the mail or something, but it was taking far too long, and it had already been seven minutes.

An uneasy feeling settled in my gut. I clenched my jaw and turned to Jaxon, whose arms were crossed, trying to stay warm.

"Have any of you seen Carmen return?" I asked while chewing on an energy bar, trying to maintain some semblance of calm.

"Nothing," he replied, his breath visible in the freezing air. We had shut off the van to save on gas without any warning that a snowstorm was coming. Axel shook his head in agreement, his gaze never leaving the house.

My worry for Carmen consumed me, growing with each passing moment.

Suddenly, the front door opened, and Logan stepped out with his pack in their shifted wolf form. *Something happened to Carmen.*

"We need to go," said Jaxon, sitting up immediately.

"Fuck, she'll know we've been watching her this whole time," I said, breathing hard.

"She could fucking die out there," Jaxon said harshly. "Every minute that's passing by..."

Axel nodded in agreement. "She won't survive long in this weather."

Jaxon sighed, frustrated. "The snow's getting worse. She could be lost out there. We need to go after her, too."

Eventually, my instincts won out, and I knew we couldn't wait any longer. "We're going after her."

We quickly stripped off our clothes and shifted into our wolf forms. I used my powerful hind legs to shut the door behind us before leading my pack out into the blizzard.

Our vision blurred as the snow lashed against our faces, making it nearly impossible to see.

"*Stay together,*" I commanded my pack telepathically.

The storm was rough, and the search was agonizingly slow because of how deep the snow was. But we were driven by the need to find Carmen and bring her to safety.

I sniffed the air, searching for her scent.

Finally, after slipping and sliding over numerous obstacles, I spotted her lying motionless in the snow, shivering and nearly buried beneath a blanket of white.

She had fallen asleep in the snow, and my heart leaped with panic.

"*Oh fuck,*" said Axel replied.

"*We're going to surround her. She needs our warmth.*"

My pack and I quickly surrounded her, using our warm bodies to provide her with much-needed heat. I draped myself over her as Axel and Jaxon pressed against her on both sides. As we pressed against her trembling form, I prayed that it would be enough to wake her.

***

Carmen

As I slowly regained consciousness, my body felt heavy and trapped.

The warmth surrounding me was comforting, but I felt something cold against my nose. Opening my eyes, I discovered heavy, warm fur on top of me and to my sides. It was like a very heavy blanket but hot as hell.

Then I smelled something familiar, like a long-forgotten memory.

"Ty...Tyler, is that you?" I stammered, my teeth chattering from the cold. I stirred, and the heavy weight on top of me shifted. I struggled to make sense of the situation, trying to reconcile my anger toward him with the familiar scent of his skin.

Wait, what the hell was he doing here with his pack?

My mind buzzed with conflicting emotions as I quickly stood between the three wolves while the wind whipped across my face.

Tyler nudged my ankle with his snout, and I swallowed. I hated him with my entire being, but I was dying out here.

Breathing hard, I looked around, realizing I didn't have many options, so I climbed onto Tyler's back. I never thought I'd feel grateful and resentful at the same time.

He raced through the streets while I clung to his back, feeling his muscles and tendons flex underneath me. Being this close to him made my face burn, and not just from the wind.

How could he still have this effect on me? I felt nothing but contempt toward him, yet being this close was eliciting even more emotions than I cared to admit.

Suddenly, he stopped in front of the house with his pack, and I was so grateful to see the house again, which had clearly been under my nose this entire time.

I climbed off his back—my body still ice-cold and trembling, making it a chore.

The three wolves shifted back, and Tyler immediately turned to me while naked, catching me leaning against a car and shivering.

"You're still cold," he said. "We need to get inside the house."

I tried to speak, but my jaw was locked tight with cold. *Oh wow, he was built.* I couldn't help but lower my gaze to his navel.

"You're not okay," he said gruffly, scooping me up in his very warm arms as I tried to protest. He quickly jogged to the front door of the house, completely naked. "Open the door, Jaxon. Don't bother knocking."

Thankfully, it was unlocked as Tyler quickly carried me inside, cradling me like a fragile treasure. He set me down on the couch. The moment we were all inside, the alphas towered over me, concern etched on their faces. I wondered where Logan and his pack were, but then I remembered him saying he would look for me after ten minutes if I didn't show up.

He was probably out there looking for me.

"Get her clothes off," Tyler ordered gruffly. "She might get hypothermia."

"Wait, what?!" I tried to protest, my teeth chattering violently from the cold. "That's crazy... I can't."

"Trust us, Carmen," Jaxon said, his voice surprisingly gentle as he knelt before me naked. "We need to warm you up quickly, or you could be in real danger. We would need to take you to a hospital to get checked."

Hating hospitals, I nodded, and Jaxon started removing my icy jacket while Axel hurried to take off my shoes, socks, and pants.

"This too," said Axel, tugging on my bra. I swallowed; it was indeed close to my skin. I couldn't even feel my hands anymore.

"Here," said Tyler, lifting me by the waist and setting me down on the living room rug. "Get the fire going, Axel."

Tyler immediately positioned himself behind me, pulling me flush against his broad chest. His skin felt like a furnace, and I couldn't help but lean in for more of that delicious warmth as I trembled.

Jaxon settled himself in front of me, pressing his firm, warm body against my breasts. "Skin to skin, baby."

"You're shivering; relax, honey," Tyler whispered into my ear. I could feel both alphas' heat seeping into me, chasing away the bone-deep chill.

"Damn it," Jaxon muttered, his warm breath brushing against my skin. "She's barely breathing. What the hell was she thinking, going out in this storm?"

"Maybe she just wanted some fresh air," Axel interjected as he turned on the electric fireplace. The glow of the flames illuminated the room, casting dancing shadows on the walls.

I would have laughed if I weren't so cold and exhausted. My body felt heavy and numb, and I struggled to form a response. All I could do was press closer to Tyler and Jaxon, silently begging for more of their life-saving warmth.

As the heat from their bodies began to thaw me, my mind wandered to dangerous territory.

I could feel Jaxon's erection pressing against the outside of my pussy, making me shiver for entirely different reasons. I hadn't worn underwear during my adventures outside, and I started to realize how exposed I was between these alphas.

If I dared to spread my legs even an inch, he would be able to penetrate me without any resistance. My thoughts were abruptly interrupted by Tyler's growing arousal, his erection nudging between my ass cheeks.

* * *

Tyler

I focused on Carmen's shivering form, gently rubbing her arms to encourage blood flow. The heat from our pressed bodies was intensifying, and I couldn't help but feel my arousal growing along with it.

As I pulled her closer, I buried my face in her soft hair, breathing in the scent that clung to her despite the cold. It was maddening, and I struggled to stifle the desire building inside me. My priority was to ensure her safety, but damn if she didn't make it difficult.

"You're getting warmer. I can feel it," I said.

"It's not too bad anymore," she whispered, her breath hitching in her throat as I took her hand resting at her side.

"Good," I growled, starting to purr. I needed to infuse the calming vibrations of my purr so she could feel completely relaxed with us.

I felt her heartbeat gradually return to normal, her once icy hand slowly warming as I wrapped mine around it. Her well-being was all that mattered, even though my own body was betraying me, my erection growing harder by the minute. Her juicy ass pressing against my dick made it challenging to think straight.

And it wasn't lost on me that she had walked outside without underwear. Jealousy stabbed through me at the thought of her sleeping with her platonic alpha friend.

Suddenly, the door crashed open—an icy gust of wind swirling into the room. Logan stormed in, his eyes blazing with fury, and I sighed, annoyed that he had to ruin our moment.

"What the hell is going on?" he demanded, his voice sharp and accusatory.

chapter 9

. . .

Tyler

Logan came to a halt when he saw Carmen, half-naked and cradled against my chest.

His nostrils flared, and I could sense his anger radiating off him in waves. I was puzzled by his anger because, as far as I knew, he hadn't marked Carmen at all or laid claim to her. I could smell her innocence. An alpha had never touched her, and I felt an overwhelming urge to protect her.

"Logan," I growled, trying to keep my voice steady. "Carmen got lost in the storm. We need to fucking warm her up."

"By stripping her down and holding her like that?" he snapped, clearly unconvinced this was a good thing for Carmen.

"I can speak for myself," Carmen said in a low voice.

"Skin-to-skin contact is the fastest way," I growled. "She was barely breathing when we found her. You should be grateful we were there to save her. Where the fuck were you?"

Logan's gaze flicked between Carmen and me, assessing the situation. He clenched his fists at his sides, his jaw tight.

For a moment, silence hung heavy in the air, the tension between us palpable. Logan's jaw tightened as he took in the scene—the fire, the discarded clothes, the intimate closeness between us. His eyes flicked over my bare chest pressed against hers, and something dark and primal flared in them.

"You call this saving her?" Logan growled, stepping closer, his fists still clenched. My eyes narrowed—I wasn't in the mood to deal with his possessive alpha bullshit right now.

Not when Carmen's life was hanging by a thread.

"Yes," I barked. "It's the only way to keep her warm. If you've got a better idea, feel free to share."

Logan's gaze shifted to Carmen's face, and the anger in his expression wavered for just a moment as concern took over. She looked so small and fragile between Jaxon and me, our bodies providing what warmth we could.

"Carmen, how are you feeling?" Logan asked, his voice softening.

"I'm fine. Guys, don't worry about me," she whispered, her voice weak from the cold. My heart clenched, realizing how fragile this omega was.

The thought that I had rejected her and broken her heart was eating me alive.

"Damn it, Carmen," Logan whispered, his voice cracking as he moved to kneel beside her, brushing a strand of hair from her face. "You should never have left."

"I'm sorry," she whispered, her voice breaking.

"Hey, don't," I cut her off gently, my voice softening despite the possessive edge that still lingered. I could sense in her voice how scared and vulnerable she felt, and I knew it wasn't the time for harsh words or alpha posturing. "You don't need to apologize. We're just glad you're safe."

"She's going to be okay," Jaxon said. "We just need to keep her warm."

Logan quickly began to remove his clothes, looking determined to do skin-to-skin with Carmen as well. I shot Jaxon a look to step aside for Logan. I was too exhausted to fight, and Carmen wasn't mine. As Jaxon moved away, Carmen held out her arms with a whimper, trying to prevent him from leaving.

"Don't worry, I'm here," said Logan, taking Jaxon's place in front of Carmen and pressing his chest against her perky breasts. She sighed in relief.

Her cold backside pressed against my thighs, prompting me to massage her cheeks to warm her up. She began to squirm, trying to get away.

"We need to do this," I told her. "Don't move, Carmen. You need to get warm."

Since she could barely talk, she nodded instead as I continued to knead her soft cheeks. She had certainly grown over the years.

As she warmed up, her omega scent became more pronounced, calling to me. I couldn't help but bury my face in her hair to savor her familiar fragrance. Carmen smelled incredible, just as she always did. As I rubbed my hand around her backside, I glanced down at her pale cheeks, which were beginning to blush with color.

Very good.

Carmen's breathing gradually steadied, and her shivering began to subside. It seemed our efforts were working, but I knew we couldn't let our guard down just yet. She was still weak, and the cold had taken its toll on her fragile omega body.

Omegas weren't built like alphas. They were the weakest gender in the wolf hierarchy and required ultimate protection.

"Thank you, both of you," Carmen whispered.

"Of course," I replied, and Logan nodded in agreement. Despite the rivalry between us, it was impossible to ignore our unspoken understanding: we would do anything for Carmen.

As I held her close, I was overwhelmed by her scent—like limes and fresh rain. The way her plump rear cradled my cock was intoxicating. My inner alpha growled possessively, but I pushed it down, reminding myself that now wasn't the time for such thoughts. Right now, all that mattered was keeping Carmen safe and warm, even if it meant sharing her with her best friend.

Carmen

MY EYES fluttered shut as I tried to manage my fast breaths, overwhelmed by a secret arousal coursing through me. I was sure they could smell it too, since I didn't have a shred of clothing on.

I was trapped between Tyler and Logan, their muscular alpha bodies pressing against mine. Tyler's erection nestled between my ass cheeks, coupled with his hand rubbing me, was more than enough to make me feel aroused, even though I hated him. But after this, I found I hated him a little less.

"Tyler, how did you know where I was?" I asked, finding it easier to speak as my shivering subsided.

"I saw you leaving the Alpha compound," he said in a low voice. "My pack and I followed you to make sure you were in a safe place."

I suddenly grimaced because it felt like my pussy couldn't stop clenching. It was a little painful, but not so much, but I attributed it to being horny.

"What's wrong, Carmen?" Logan asked, sensing my distress. I gave him a worried look, unsure of how to put my fears into words.

"I think... I might be nearing my heat," I admitted

between gasps. "My... err, pussy keeps clenching. I've never had that happen before."

"It could also just be you getting warmer," Tyler said as he stiffened behind me.

I hoped he was right because the pins-and-needles sensation spreading across my body was making it hard to think about anything else. But as Logan shifted closer, I could feel his arousal pressing against me, and I blushed furiously. I knew my face had to be red as hell by now.

"Can't you two keep your manhoods in check?" I asked, trying to lighten the mood. Tyler laughed, while Logan chuckled and shook his head.

"Impossible when I'm holding a beautiful omega like you," Logan teased, making my blush deepen. Tyler's large hands rubbed my shoulders, and I couldn't deny that I was feeling warmer.

Through half-lidded eyes, I saw Axel and Griffin busy themselves in the kitchen, making hot chocolate while Jaxon shoved his clothes back on. The frustration in Jaxon's eyes brought back memories of our time in the fitting room, making me squirm between the two giant pack leaders.

"Are you uncomfortable?" Logan observed, his voice filled with concern.

"Yes, but I need to get up, or I'll go into heat right here," I said, swallowing hard.

As I stood up in the middle of the living room, Griffin's gaze traveled down my naked body, lingering on the patch of dark hair between my legs.

My cheeks burned, and I felt painfully aware of the six alphas in the house all watching me. Talon seemed to anticipate this moment because he appeared with a set of pajamas and socks for me.

"Here, I grabbed these from your suitcase," Talon said,

handing me the clothes. As our hands brushed, the slightest touch sent tingles shooting through me.

"Thank you," I managed to say breathlessly, biting my lip as I struggled to put the clothes on. My muscles still felt weak, betraying me at every turn.

"Let me help you," Griffin offered, coming over and gently assisting me with putting the clothes on. His nearness and warmth only heightened my sensitivity, making it harder to resist the pull of my heat.

LATER, I was sitting on the couch between Griffin and Talon, wrapped in a huge blanket, before the roaring fireplace. The warmth of their bodies on either side of me was both comforting and overwhelming.

"Thank you," I said quietly to the alphas surrounding me, my voice shaking with emotion. "All of you... for saving my life. I shouldn't have ever left."

"It's fine," said Griffin, rubbing my arm, and I welcomed his touch. "You're safe and sound now with us. Just don't run off again, sweetheart. You had us all worried for a second there, babe."

I giggled as Axel handed me a steaming mug of hot cocoa. I took it gratefully, wrapping my hands around the warm ceramic.

Logan turned on the television, flipping through the channels until he found the news. A serious-looking newscaster appeared on the screen, her expression grave.

"Residents are advised to stay indoors at all costs, as heavy snowfall and strong winds are expected to continue throughout the night. Emergency services are currently unable to predict when the storm will end, and you may not receive help in time. Please stay indoors."

As the alphas began discussing our dire situation, I couldn't help but feel a little worried for myself. These were six powerful, dominant alphas, fully grown and exuding raw strength, trapped with me in this home. My heart raced as I contemplated being confined with them, unsure of how long we would be stuck together.

I glanced around the room, trying to distract myself from the overwhelming thoughts. But every time my eyes landed on one of the alphas, my mind wandered to forbidden fantasies, images of each alpha taking me and claiming me as their own.

Heat pooled between my legs, my body betraying me as I felt my heat approaching. This wasn't just a fleeting moment of freezing before thawing out.

It had to be my heat.

Taking a sip of the hot cocoa, I felt the warmth slide down my throat, intensifying the fire already burning within me. My body craved something cool, anything to douse the flames threatening to engulf me. Grimacing, I handed back the mug and tried to push away the desperate need coursing through me.

But it was no use. The first signs of my heat were unfolding.

It felt like a fire of warmth pulsing in my core before spreading throughout my body. My breath quickened, and my skin became hypersensitive to even the slightest touch. Clutching the arm of the chair with white knuckles, I fought against the rising heat, knowing I was just moments away from being entirely consumed by the pain.

Not here. Not now. Not with two packs who weren't even mine.

The thought of being so vulnerable in front of Tyler, the alpha who had cruelly rejected me all those years ago, filled me with dread. Memories of his cold dismissal flooded back, how he looked at me with disdain and told me I wasn't good enough for him. The pain of that rejection still lingered deep in my heart, and now, being trapped in this cabin with him felt like an open wound.

Across the room, Logan's keen gaze never left me.

He always seemed to sense when something was off with me, and now was no different. His eyes flickered with concern as he picked up on my discomfort.

chapter 10

. . .

Logan

Carmen shifted uncomfortably in her chair.

Her scent was stronger, and I sensed she might be right after all—she was going into heat in a house full of alphas.

I walked over to her, keeping my gaze locked on hers as I sat beside her.

"Carmen?" I said, trying to sound casual while my heart raced. She looked up at me, her green eyes wide and nervous. I knelt before her, my gaze never leaving hers. "You're starting your heat, aren't you?"

Carmen bit her lip and nodded, her cheeks flushed with embarrassment.

"This is a disaster," she whispered, looking down.

Her hands trembled in her lap, and a low whimper escaped her throat. I couldn't bear the thought of her suffering through her heat alone, especially without a pack to support her.

A deep, primal need to protect her surged within me.

But Tyler's presence complicated everything, and I knew

she still cared for him. The possessive flare in my chest was hard to ignore.

I wanted her, but I had always respected our friendship.

"Remember, we're here. You have six alphas at your beck and call," I reminded her. "We'll help you if it comes down to that."

"Logan," she whispered shakily, holding her belly. "If we do this... it'll change everything between us."

"I know," I replied gently, my jaw tightening. "But I've never been more certain about anything in my life. You don't have to go through this alone, Carmen. I'm here for you."

Her uncertain gaze flicked over to Tyler, who stood across the room with his arms crossed, looking tense and jealous. A look of hurt flickered across her face as he quickly averted his gaze from her. She looked back at me, and I felt a surge of sympathy and protectiveness wash over me.

I wanted to shield her from the pain and wrap her in warmth and safety.

"I don't know," she said before crying out in pain as she curled onto the floor.

Panic surged within me as I followed her to the ground.

"Listen to me," I said passionately, placing my hand on her shoulder. "I've wanted you for years, but I never pushed you because I respected our friendship. Now, though, I can't stand by and do nothing while you're in pain. You will need my knot to get through this heat, and I'm here for you. I'll take responsibility for everything, especially if you get pregnant. You'll need to trust me, Carmen."

"Okay," she whispered, her voice barely audible. With that simple word, I quickly scooped her up in my arms.

"What's going on?" Tyler demanded sharply.

"She's in heat," I barked. "Not that you care."

His eyes flickered as he leaned back in his chair. I shot a warning glance at Tyler, daring him to challenge my claim on

Carmen. But he remained rooted to the spot, his fists clenched at his sides, battling some internal demon that threatened to tear him apart.

Carmen gasped in my arms, the pain in her middle intensifying.

As a natural impulse, her gaze flickered to Tyler, who stood abruptly, casting a tall, brooding shadow over the room. His eyes, usually so controlled, were dark and stormy as they bore into Carmen's very soul. The electricity between them crackled and sizzled, their connection undeniable even in this tense situation.

"Tyler..." Carmen breathed, her voice barely audible. Her eyes met his for just a moment, and the hurt from years ago flashed across her face. My heart ached for her, but I wasn't going to allow Tyler to play games with her anymore.

Carmen

MY HEART RACED with uncertainty as I locked eyes with Tyler. But his next words broke me.

"I'll stay out of your way," Tyler said gruffly to Logan, his voice strained. "You don't need me for this."

My heart clenched painfully at his harsh dismissal, feeling as though a fresh wound had reopened. Bitterness bubbled up inside me, threatening to consume every ounce of my strength. *Why did it feel like his rejection was cutting me open all over again?*

Tyler turned away, and I was shocked—especially after our skin-to-skin session and feeling his arousal press up against me during it all.

I thought he wanted me.

"That's fine," Logan said, quickly carrying me into the

bedroom. Once there, my body felt as if it were engulfed in flames. My skin burned, every nerve alive and screaming for relief as I writhed in discomfort on the bed.

"I changed my mind," I gasped. "I'll wait until this passes. I can handle this."

"Carmen, you can't be serious," Logan said worriedly, placing a hand on my knee as slick gushed into my pajama pants. "You're not alone anymore."

Logan was here. He had always been here, a constant presence in my life. But the sting of Tyler's cold rejection reminded me that I wasn't worth it. There was something wrong with me.

"Logan, please," I sobbed, tears streaming down my cheeks. "Please leave."

"Absolutely not," Logan replied firmly. "Carmen, you could die from your heat if you don't allow me to knot you."

I shook my head, adamant in my refusal. "Leave with your pack. Get me some pain medicine. I'll make it through this."

Logan's jaw clenched, and I could tell he was far from happy with my decision. "Carmen, it's not that simple. You know what can happen in just a few hours."

"I know," I begged, my voice barely a whisper. I would call him if I couldn't handle it anymore. But I just needed some time to process everything. "I promise I'll let you know if it's too much."

He sighed loudly, not moving for a long moment. Finally, he nodded, scooting off the bed. "Alright. But we'll be back to check on you."

"Okay," I whimpered as he left the room along with Griffin and Talon.

As soon as the door clicked shut behind them, I quickly bolted from the bed and locked the door. My body was on fire, and I knew this was only going to get worse.

What if I *could* survive this? I had never actually heard of an omega dying from being in heat.

A searing, intense pain ripped through my abdomen, causing me to gasp and clutch at my stomach.

My entire body trembled with a sensation that was both agonizing and pleasurable. I felt hot wetness dripping down my thighs and pooling on the sheets beneath me. Desperately, I reached between my legs, trying to find some release from the pulsing ache within me.

I shoved my hand down my leggings, feeling my slick folds as I attempted to finger myself. I needed something thick inside me.

This wasn't working at all.

I tried to push my finger in, but a barrier stopped me, and it was painful to keep going.

"Oh my god," I said out loud as hot tears rolled down my face.

With a frustrated grunt, I kicked away the blankets and continued to writhe on the bed, unable to ease the relentless throbbing in my core.

It felt like I was locked within my own body, a prisoner to my heat and the torment it brought. I whimpered, crying on the bed as the heat fully took hold of me.

chapter 11

. . .

Tyler

"Why are you back here?" I asked when I saw Logan and his pack walking into the living room. They were supposed to be with Carmen, knotting her despite my jealousy.

"She doesn't want anyone," said Logan, rubbing his face as he sighed.

"She needs an alpha's knot right now," I said, feeling uneasy as I stood up from my chair.

Logan ran a hand through his hair. "She doesn't want anyone, Tyler. She's refusing us all after you acted like an ass."

Anger and confusion twisted in my stomach. "That's not supposed to happen! You guys are supposed to knot her during her heat."

"Look, she just doesn't want it," Logan shot back, his dark eyes narrowing.

"Then what the hell do you plan on doing?" I demanded, clenching my fists as I paced the living room.

His face reddened with anger as he confronted me, his voice low and dangerous. "The only alpha she wants is you. So, fucking grow some balls and stop rejecting her constantly!"

My jaw tightened, but I didn't respond, still pacing the living room like a caged animal. Axel, ever the voice of reason, stepped closer. "Tyler, we really should help Carmen. How would you feel if something happened to her?"

An intense pressure squeezed my chest. I couldn't lead her on, but I also couldn't let anything happen to her.

"I wouldn't be able to live with myself," I admitted, my voice cracking slightly.

Suddenly, we all heard a heart-stopping shriek coming from Carmen's room. Panic surged through me, and I sprinted toward her door.

"Carmen... open up!" I shouted, pounding on the locked door. Adrenaline pumped through my veins, making me forget that I was only wearing boxers.

"Absolutely not!" Carmen's defiant voice came from behind the door. But I could hear the fear in her tone and how she was getting weaker by the second.

"Dammit, Carmen, you're in heat," I growled through the door. "You need an alpha's knot. Let Logan help you."

"No, thank you," she replied primly, but I could hear her grunting in pain.

"Are you still a virgin?" I asked gently, trying to calm her down. There was silence, and I knew I'd struck a nerve. "I'll be gentle for your first time."

"Get lost, Tyler!" she screamed.

My patience snapped.

"I will break this door down if I have to!" I snarled. Hearing the sound of the window opening, I realized with horror that she might try to throw herself out into the snow again.

She wasn't going to freeze again—not on my watch.

Carmen

MY HEART ACHED as I listened to Tyler's words from behind the closed door. I couldn't trust him again, yet his sweet words pulled at me, making my body ache for him even more. My belly throbbed with pain from my heat, and I wanted nothing more than to have an alpha's knot inside of me.

Especially Tyler's knot, but he despised me.

Desperate to escape, I fumbled with the cold window screen, my fingers burning from the freezing metal.

The door suddenly burst open. I turned, taking a deep breath, and saw Tyler standing there, his eyes blazing with fury and desire.

"I don't want you," I yelled. "I got over you a long time ago."

But he was already across the room in a few long strides, the floors shaking with his force. His instincts as an alpha had taken over, and it was clear he needed to make sure I knew who I belonged to. Tyler's eyes locked on mine, and the anger within him morphed into something darker, more possessive.

He stepped toward me while I stood at the window—my heart pounding like crazy, while my middle burned.

"I can't let you do this," he growled, his voice low and dangerous. "You can't hurt yourself again."

I stared up at him, my chest heaving as I fought against the heat that threatened to undo me.

"I'll get by just fine. Why don't you go back to the compound to serve Henry?" I snapped, even though every fiber of my being screamed for him.

"Don't be stubborn, honey. I can't stand by and watch you suffer like this. I'll do whatever it takes to help you through your heat."

"Even if it means breaking my heart again?" I asked, tears prickling at the corners of my eyes.

"Never again," Tyler promised, his gaze softening as he took my cold hands in his. "I won't leave you this time. Let me prove it to you."

As much as I wanted to believe him, the fear of being hurt again held me back. But the pain from my heat was unbearable, and I found myself relenting as he led me toward the warm bed.

Tyler's grip on my wrist was firm, pulling me to him with intensity. His scent of smoky cedarwood with a hint of leather enveloped me, making my knees weak and my heart race. I tried to tell myself I hated him, but my body betrayed me as I hugged him back.

"I never should have let you go," Tyler confessed, his voice raw with emotion as he hugged me tighter on the bed, his erection pressing against my leg. "And I'm not going to make that mistake again."

"Tyler, you can't just waltz back into my life and expect everything to be okay," I said, worried, just in case.

"Watch me," he growled, pressing his lean, muscular body against mine. The heat emanating from him made my skin tingle, and the desire pooling in my core became nearly unbearable. "I won't ever let you go again."

He helped remove my sticky clothes from my body, my heart racing for it all to be off. Then he gazed at my bare breasts, running his hand gently down my belly.

Tyler had never seen me naked, even while we dated before. His eyes took on a deeper shade than usual as he gazed at my body from head to toe while I lay there on my back.

"What is it?" I asked, swallowing hard and feeling very shy before him as my thighs stayed clenched together.

"So fucking beautiful," he said simply as his hand made

contact with my pussy. "You're so wet for me, Carmen. But we need to make sure you're ready."

He squeezed my pussy, and my arousal spiked. I could barely contain my moans as Jaxon shut the window. All my focus was on Tyler.

The alpha inhaled deeply, taking in the scent of my arousal as his wolfish yellow eyes glowed in the dark. He scared me, but the hunger in them also stirred something primal within me. This was what I'd always dreamt of but never dared believe would happen.

"God, I can't believe you waited for me," he murmured with admiration as he squeezed my pussy again. "Your virgin pussy is all mine."

I gripped the sheets nervously as he massaged my thighs apart. I was anxious about that since my thighs jiggled a lot, but he didn't seem to notice as he kissed my thighs with slow, tender care. I started to calm down a little because of how gentle he was, and I ran my hand through his dark wavy hair as he kissed the top of my pussy next.

"I need you," I said, my pussy clenching with need. I had never been this wet before in my life, and I was more than ready to take him inside me even though it would be my first time getting knotted. As he licked my sensitive folds in long strokes, I couldn't help but moan. "Tyler, it feels so good... but I need your knot. It hurts."

"Alright, love," he grinned wickedly as he pumped his cock twice, its thick girth making my mouth water. He spread my thighs wider, and I was so horny for him that I just wanted him to plunge into me already.

"Oh my goodness," I said as more slick seeped down my pussy. My heart started to beat faster.

"Ready?" he asked, his voice low and seductive. "This will hurt a bit since you're a virgin."

As his cock pressed agonizingly slow against my entrance,

my belly clenched with need. The thought of carrying his child both scared and excited me, but with Tyler's promise echoing in my ears, I decided to trust him.

"Please," I begged. "Fill me up. I need you. I'm not going to break."

He pushed inside me, his deep groan mingling with my scream as he took my virginity. The sharp pain soon gave way to pleasure as he began to thrust powerfully inside me, stretching me deliciously around his girth.

chapter 12

. . .

Tyler

"Yes, scream for me, baby," I growled into my omega's ear as I took her virginity. The pleasure of claiming Carmen, an omega I had loved for years, was unparalleled.

It was the most incredible night of my life.

"Oh my God," she gasped, moaning beneath me. I covered her mouth with mine, savoring her moans as I thrust into her virgin pussy.

"You are mine. All mine."

Carmen's thighs trembled as I strained to enter her tight channel. Her slickness coated my dick, providing just enough lubrication as I thrust faster.

"Please, more," she begged, the sheets tangling around her voluptuous hips. Sweat glistened on her flushed face as she moaned in pleasure, her breasts bouncing with every pump of my cock.

"You look like a fucking princess," I rasped, quickening my pace to give her the pleasure and relief she craved from my knot.

The arch of her back accentuated every curve of her body.

With each powerful thrust of mine, her mouth would open a little driving me fucking wild.

"Oh, do I?" she moaned as I sucked on the skin of her collarbone.

"Let's make that *queen* then," I said, thrusting one last powerful time. My cock began to swell rapidly as I released inside her. She screamed, her eyes widening at the sensation of my knot for the first time. "My queen."

My feelings for her surged as the euphoria of knotting the omega I had desired for years coursed through me. Her moans fueled my desire as I growled and claimed her as mine with my knot.

"Oh my God."

"We should have fucked a long time ago," I declared. "Years and years ago."

"And whose fault is that?" she asked, shaking her head with a small smile. I knew she was right. It was all my fucking fault that we hadn't been together sooner, but I had done it for her safety.

***

Carmen

I FINALLY FELT RELIEF. The fire in my belly subsided as Tyler's semen filled me. It was hot and intense, making me feel closer to him than ever before. I blushed when he touched my face lovingly, his gaze soft as he looked at me.

"Nothing can erase the pain of what I did to you," Tyler whispered. "But I promise you, I'll make up for all the lost time."

I stroked his chest, and he tenderly brushed my hair back with his fingers, deepening our connection.

"What if I get pregnant?" I asked, a bit worried since I wasn't sure how committed he was to me yet.

"I've always dreamt of having a baby with you—dreams I never got to tell you about," he replied, his voice filled with emotion. I blushed again. He suddenly kissed me on the lips, leaving me breathless when it ended.

I was so conflicted.

Was he serious about me or just playing with my feelings again? The rejection had happened years ago—maybe he had finally grown up.

I lay there knotted to Tyler for a good half hour while Jaxon and Axel joined us on the bed.

"I never thought I would get knotted by you—out of all people," I blurted out, looking at Tyler as he gazed at me lazily, his eyes half-lidded with desire.

"Agreed," he said, touching my breasts as we lay entwined in each other's arms. "Never thought I would have the honor of taking your virginity."

"Lucky bastard," Jaxon chimed in, clearly voicing his jealousy and wishing to be the one to take my virginity.

When Tyler's knot deflated and released me, I felt the soreness of my pussy. The fire of pain in my belly started to intensify when he pulled away.

"Damn, the heat doesn't let up," I said as sweat streaked down my back.

"Jaxon will knot you now," said Tyler, and I nodded, turning towards the next alpha waiting. Jaxon was prepared, and my eyes widened when I saw his massive cock, streaked with angry purple veins. Jaxon's shaggy brown hair framed our faces, shielding us from anyone's view as he climbed on top of me.

"Ready, baby?"

"Yes, Jax."

He immediately pushed his dick into me without delay,

and I gasped when I felt him pulsing inside of me. I grabbed hold of his thick arms, which flexed beneath my fingers as he pushed deep inside me.

"Does that feel good, baby?"

"It does," I moaned, enjoying every inch of his cock sliding into my writhing, heat-ridden body. I never realized that I would need these alphas like air itself.

⸻

Tyler

I couldn't help but smile as I watched Carmen getting fucked by Jaxon. Her thin pussy lips hugged his cock tightly, glistening with her arousal.

The sight was unexpectedly erotic, and I found myself growing hard again.

"Fuck," I muttered under my breath, pulling on my jeans just in time for my cell phone to ring. Glancing at the screen, I saw Henry's name flash before me.

With a sigh, I left the room to take the call.

"Where the hell are you, Tyler?" Henry barked as soon as I answered. "You're head of security—you can't just disappear whenever you want."

"Relax," I replied, trying to sound casual. "I'm taking a break. I'll be back tomorrow."

I needed more time with Carmen to figure out how our lives would be together because I was never going to leave her again.

"Have you seen Carmen?" Henry asked, his voice tense.

"Uh, no," I lied, my heart suddenly pounding in my chest. "Why?"

"Hmm...I'll ask the guards at border patrol. They'll find her."

My mind raced, knowing immediately that Henry wasn't going to let go of her or forget about her anytime soon. I needed to get back to the compound and appease him.

"I'll be at the compound tomorrow and help you look for her," I said in a low voice. This was too much. I couldn't break her heart again.

"Fine," he snapped. "When you find her, remember she's going to be my bride. Have you smelled her scent yet? It's intoxicating."

The conversation suddenly felt suffocating, and I hung up, my thoughts racing. I couldn't ignore the fact that I worked too closely with Henry, and Carmen would never truly be safe with me. My heart ached at the thought of letting her go, but I knew it was the best thing for her.

Walking into the living room, I saw Logan and his pack sitting there, looking dejected. They were going to be happy as hell once I told them the news that my pack and I were leaving.

"Logan," I said, sighing as I sat across from him. The sounds of Carmen moaning and Jaxon grunting were unmistakable.

"What is it?" Logan asked, his jaw tense from being rejected by Carmen.

"I have to leave," I said.

"What the fuck, man? Carmen's going to be pissed."

"Henry's looking for her," I replied. "I need to be back at the compound by tomorrow, or else he's going to suspect something."

I couldn't bring myself to say the next words because even I couldn't take it anymore. My heart hurt at the thought of letting go of Carmen forever. If I officially rejected her again, she would never forgive me. But I had to say goodbye, even if it hurt.

"So what does that mean for you and Carmen?" Talon asked.

"It'll be over," I said, letting out a long, shuddering breath while the stabbing feeling in my chest grew sharper. Even though the pain was emotional, it felt real, and every vein in my body rebelled against leaving her. When I was around her, I was happy, even though she didn't trust me.

Everything about her sang to me. She was mine—my mate.

"What?"

"Look, it's for her safety," I growled. "Please take care of her. Don't ever bring her back to the alpha compound. I know you care for her, Logan."

Logan's face looked stern as he nodded. He clearly wasn't happy about the prospect of dealing with a rejected omega.

As I walked back to the bedroom, I paused multiple times, trying to think of another way we could be together. Carmen would never be safe if I chose to stay with her. Henry was completely enamored with her.

I needed to divert his efforts for now.

Building up my resolve, I twisted the doorknob and walked in, seeing Carmen entangled with Jaxon. Her face was flushed, and her stunning, thick thigh was wrapped around his waist. My breath caught in my throat at the sight of her. Axel lay on her other side, waiting for his turn to knot her. The poor bloke would, unfortunately, never get his taste of her.

I couldn't do this. But I had to do it.

Jaxon's knot released her, and they both turned to me. She sensed that something was obviously off with me, even though I tried to keep a cordial smile on my face to mask my inner turmoil about letting her go.

"Tyler, what's wrong?" she asked in a soft voice.

She knew something was wrong.

"Everything was a mistake between us," I said, breathing hard, feeling the lie spill from my mouth so easily.

Her face paled instantly. "What do you mean?"

"I wasn't thinking clearly when I saw that you were in heat," I said coldly, my heart shattering at the vulnerability in her gaze. She looked so innocent as her expression began to crack. I had to get the hell out of here before I took her in my arms and told her that it wasn't how I really felt.

"But you said..."

"It was all fake," I said, looking away. I couldn't bear to see her face breaking at the sight of me. She was already starting to hate me, and I could feel it. "We need to leave, guys."

chapter 13

. . .

Carmen

This couldn't be happening again.

I grabbed the blanket, pulling it up to my chest as I sat up from the fog of my heat. Confusion whirled through my mind as I stared at Tyler's face, searching for answers. I thought we were fine, but apparently, he wasn't happy with me.

"Why?" I asked simply. "Am I not good enough? Please, just tell me the answer to that, and I will never ask again."

Instead, he coldly turned away from me. "It's nothing to do with you, Carmen."

"Dude, what the fuck?!" roared Jaxon, his hand resting on the small of my back.

"Logan will take care of you, Carmen," said Tyler, leaving me at a loss for words. I was too shell-shocked to respond. He suddenly stormed over to me and lifted my chin with a rough hand. Tears spilled down my face as he looked at me. "Let him knot you, okay? He cares for you, and he will treat you better than I ever could."

"No," I said, my voice shuddering. "We're friends. There's nothing between us, so you don't have to worry."

"Logan will knot you," he said, his voice firm, tinged with the alpha bark that injected urgency into his words. I could tell he didn't want Logan to knot me, judging by the angry look in his gaze, but I wasn't sure. "Say yes."

"Fine," I said, just to make him leave me alone. If he didn't want to tell me what was wrong with our relationship, I didn't want to see him again.

"Good," he said, wiping away my tears. "Don't think of me again. This is the last time you'll ever see me."

"Bye," I said without another word. I had no idea why he was rejecting me again, but I didn't want the experience to be as brutal as last time.

My heart ached as he shifted into his werewolf form, landing on the floor and rushing out of the house into the snow.

"I'm so sorry," said Axel, his gaze forlorn as he stood at the door.

"It's fine," I said, even though it wasn't. Not at all. My soul was crumpling and dying at having let Tyler take my virginity. Letting him have all of me, even for a moment, was a disaster.

"It's a fucked-up decision. We'll be back for you, because this isn't goodbye," said Jaxon determinedly before he shifted and followed his pack leader. He didn't want to say goodbye, but he looked back one last time before leaving, his eyes lost.

"Bye, Axel," I said, turning to the gentle giant who didn't pressure me for anything.

"Bye, sweetheart," he said, breathing hard, before turning to follow his pack.

When they all left, I crumpled into the bed, crying from the painful stabbing sensation in my heart, combined with the discomfort from my heat.

My world felt like it was shattering again. The abyss of depression that I had fallen into during Tyler's first rejection loomed close as I gasped for air.

The pillow was drenched with my tears as I lay face down on the bed, crying and covered in blankets despite running a high temperature.

"Carmen?" Logan's voice broke through my thoughts, and I felt the bed compress as he sat beside me. My tears had dried under the heat on my skin, and I looked toward him, my eyes burning. "I'm so sorry, sweetheart."

I swallowed as the heat consumed my body, begging me to take a knot.

Any knot.

"I don't want to talk about Tyler," I said, feeling anger rise in my belly at the mere thought of him. I never wanted to see him again. "I just need to be knotted right now."

His eyes widened at how easily I was giving in.

"The pain of it will pass, Carmen," he said, rubbing my back. "I don't want you to make these decisions while you're angry."

"I'm in heat, though," I said, biting my lip as I felt the burning course through my thighs and my clenching pussy. "And I like you. I've always liked you, but I didn't want to ruin our friendship."

"It won't," Logan replied, clasping my hand. "It will only make it stronger. I've always had feelings for you. I just want you to know that, Carmen."

"That's good to know," I whispered, my voice hoarse from crying. "I want to lose myself in being knotted by you all."

With that, Logan leaned in and kissed me tenderly, our lips meeting for the first time.

To my surprise, I found the sensation intoxicating, and I eagerly deepened the kiss. Our tongues danced together as arousal blossomed within me, my body responding to Logan's touch even as my heart ached from the recent rejection.

When he pulled away, he smiled, and I couldn't help but smile back at his goofy expression.

"Are you ready for my knot?" he asked, mockingly deepening his voice, and I couldn't help but giggle.

"I'm so ready," I said, turning to Griffin and Talon, who were standing at the edge of the bed. "You can join too, you know."

"I just wanted to make sure you were comfortable," Griffin said, immediately hopping onto the bed on my other side, with Talon following suit.

"I am, don't worry," I said, gritting my teeth as the pain spiked in my belly. In my desperation, I quickly turned to Logan and started unzipping his jeans, revealing his massive erection. My eyes widened at the sight of him.

He immediately picked me up and turned me around, whispering in my ear, "I want you on your knees, sweetheart."

I obeyed without hesitation, my breasts swaying as Griffin reached out to massage them. He flicked a finger over my nipples, stimulating me even more.

I refused to dwell on Tyler's rejection. I would focus on the here and now with the alphas who clearly wanted me in their lives.

Talon's fingers traced the curve of my neck, his voice husky as he whispered, "Your neck is so beautiful, Carmen. I can't wait to sink my teeth into it."

"Wait, I don't know about getting marked so early in our relationship. It's only been ten minutes since we got together."

As the words left my lips, Logan's cock slammed into my pussy from behind, making me gasp at the sudden, intense impact of pleasure.

"Enough talking," he growled, his voice thick with arousal.

"It's time for some good knotting. Let me give you relief, baby."

My pussy clenched tightly around him as I gleefully accepted his cock inside me. Logan began to thrust into me urgently as I lifted my hips to take him in deeper.

"That's a good girl," said Talon, creepily watching my every move. "You like our pack leader's dick deep in your tiny pussy, don't you?"

"Touch yourself, Carmen," commanded Logan, and my breathing grew ragged.

I reached between my legs as Logan pumped from behind, but Talon pushed my hand away so he could take over. Talon's fingers started rubbing my clit. It was a whole different sensation to have three enormous males touching me without me having to do anything except enjoy the pleasure.

This was what being an omega was about.

The sensations were overwhelming, and I couldn't help but gasp as Logan's thick cock stretched my pussy wide open.

As Logan continued to pound into me, Griffin and Talon played with my body, their touches driving me insane.

"So fucking soft," said Griffin, squeezing my breasts and sucking on my nipples.

"Our omega's clit is swollen," observed Talon, rubbing me faster with two fingers.

"Oh," I screamed when I felt my stomach muscles flex as I climaxed from Talon's expert fingering. "Oh, stop!"

"You sure?" said Talon in a soft voice, prolonging my orgasm as I moaned.

"Fuck," said Logan, thrusting deep into me as he exploded, filling me with his hot seed. I knew what to expect this time, and I braced myself as his dick knotted to me almost instantly.

"Oh my god," I moaned as I collapsed onto my belly with Logan pressed onto my back, his cock deep inside of me. His hot rapid breaths on the back of my neck made my pussy clench around him.

"If your pussy keeps clenching like that, I would never pull out even when my knot goes down," said Logan, kissing my skin.

"Don't then," I said, enjoying the feeling so much.

"Then tonight, I'll keep my cock inside your little pussy while you're sleeping. How does that sound?"

Excitement coursed through me at the thought, and I swallowed as a new wave of arousal strummed through me. "We can try that."

MY BODY still trembled with the aftershocks of my orgasm when I felt Logan's knot finally release me. As he gently slid out, I turned to face him and pressed my lips against his in a tender kiss, our breaths mingling in the heated air between us.

"God, that was amazing," I whispered, staring into his dark eyes. "But this bed is so gross."

I glanced at the damp sheets, remnants of Tyler's presence still lingering. I wanted to erase any trace of him because I was done waiting for him.

"What is it, baby?"

"I want to get rid of the mattress or move to another room," I said quickly.

"Whatever you want, Carmen. We'll take care of it," Logan quickly reassured me, his voice firm.

"Thank you," I sighed. "I really need a shower right now, though. But everything hurts."

I had never felt so sticky in all my life, just after two knottings. I also craved a nest, but that would have to wait because I desperately needed to get clean.

"I can help you, babe," said Griffin, who had been

watching me silently, and I nodded. His strong arms scooped me up effortlessly from the bed like I weighed nothing at all, though I knew I was pretty heavy.

"You're strong," I said, looking at his hairy arms flexing.

"Oh, this is nothing," he said, dismissing my concerns.

"I just never thought my heat would make my body weak like this," I admitted, feeling vulnerable in Griffin's arms.

"Don't worry," he chuckled warmly. "We'll take good care of you."

As he carried me toward the bathroom, I couldn't help but reflect on how gentle and attentive the alphas had been toward me despite our lack of familiarity. I had been friends with Logan forever, but I was still new to Griffin and Talon. Yet they all made me feel safe—a feeling I hadn't experienced since my fathers walked out on my mom.

The blue bathroom tiles were refreshingly cool beneath my feet as Griffin set me down. With one hand, he turned on the tub, adjusting the water temperature while I leaned against the counter for support.

"Please tell me that's not hot water," I pleaded, already feeling the sweltering heat of my body threatening to overwhelm me again.

"No, it's not," Griffin assured me.

"Thanks," I breathed, watching the tub fill. "I thought I was ready to get out of bed, but now I'm worried it's too soon."

"Maybe I could knot you right here while we wait for the tub to fill up," Griffin suggested, his voice low. "Then we can sit in the water together."

Tingles coursed through my body at the idea; I was already craving the connection and relief that knotting would provide.

"That sounds... wonderful," I squeaked, watching him shed his clothes at record speed. He stood before me, naked and covered in pure muscle. The dark shadow of his jaw and his tousled jet-black hair made him incredibly attractive. He literally looked like alpha perfection.

Griffin didn't waste time. He quickly pulled me against his firm chest, and I wrapped my legs around his waist. He pinned me against the cool, smooth tile floor as he slowly pushed himself inside me.

"Are you okay?" he asked.

"More than okay," I said, swallowing. This felt so good, especially since two alphas had already stretched me. The soreness I had felt since losing my virginity to Tyler seemed to disappear quickly, and maybe that was just an omega thing because no one had told me about that.

"Good girl," he said as he slowly thrust into my pussy. His cock stretched me so wonderfully that I moaned against his mouth. Our skin pressed against one another, enhancing the incredible sensation I felt all across my body.

His thrusts felt so fucking good as I gasped from his movements.

"Oh my moons," I moaned when he pistoned into me, and I clawed at his back to pull him in deeper.

"Fuck," he growled as he pulled back and into my pussy. He pumped into me one last time before finally climaxing with a roar.

chapter 14

. . .

Carmen

"Oh yes," Griffin growled as his knot swelled, stretching me even further. I widened my legs to take him in more easily. "Yes, just like that. So beautiful."

Our lips locked together as he carried me to the bathtub, my legs wrapped around his waist. It felt so good whenever his knot would jiggle inside me with my thighs clamped tight around his muscular body.

"The water feels amazing," I sighed against his mouth as he reached over to turn off the faucet. The fire of my heat was finally doused with his fluids, and it felt incredible.

"God, omega," he growled in my ear, his voice thick with lust. "You have no idea how good it feels to be inside you like this."

I moaned, feeling my arousal spike again at his words as his hard cock locked firmly inside me. "And I love it when you're inside me. I didn't think anything could take my mind off the pain, but this feels so good."

He began massaging my back, rubbing away any lingering tension and discomfort from my heat.

I could hardly move, feeling limp as I rested my chin

against his shoulder while he washed me. Alphas seemed to possess incredible strength; he wasn't tired at all after his orgasm.

"We can just sit in the water like this," I suggested, wanting him to relax.

"I'm good. Let me wash you, baby," he replied. I sighed as he massaged my back with soap. I reached up to touch his dark stubble, struck by how attractive he looked in the dim lighting of the bathroom. Somehow, he became even hotter after he knotted me.

He washed my armpits next, causing me to yelp as I tried to pull away.

"I can wash my own armpits," I said, embarrassed, but he held my arm up, staring at the small growth of dark hair.

"Relax, baby," he said, washing me thoroughly with a bubbly hand, taking care to tickle me in the process.

"Oh my god, stop," I laughed, trying to pull away, but he seemed to get even harder inside me as he continued to play with me.

"Time for a little shave," he said, taking a razor from the wall. "Be a good omega and hold still for me, please."

"No way," I objected, trying to move away, but his cock held me tightly in place as he kept my arm extended. My pussy throbbed from the intimacy of the moment.

"Stay still, babe," he instructed.

He lifted my arm again, exposing my armpit. I protested, feeling embarrassed, but his grip was unyielding.

"Let me shave you," he whispered with a wicked grin, his voice low and seductive.

"I don't want to make you do any work," I replied, grasping for any leverage as he held my arm up, running his fingers through the tiny dark hairs.

"I want to do this. It's no trouble at all, baby."

I could feel his heart thumping against mine as he pulled

me even closer. My face heated when he began to shave. For some reason, I was more sensitive to the razor since he was the one shaving me. It never felt so sexual when I was alone in the shower, hurriedly wanting to get out.

"Oh fuck," I groaned as he slid the shaver vertically, causing goosebumps to rise on every inch of my arm.

"Does that feel good, baby? We're almost done here—then we'll get to your other arm," he promised.

My body quivered under his touch as he slowly and sensually shaved my armpits, our bodies still intimately connected. As he carefully rinsed the area clean, I felt a twinge of embarrassment, my cheeks flushing red hot. But beneath it all was a sense of surrender to his dominance, igniting a primal desire within me.

"Are you done?" I asked, trying to stay annoyed with him, but his twitching cock inside me changed my mind. He was genuinely excited to shave me, which I couldn't understand, but it made my pussy twitch in response.

"All done," he whispered into my ear after putting away the shaver. He lightly bit my earlobe, and I moaned against his shoulder.

"Thank you," I said quietly, even though the whole thing was embarrassing. But he had washed and taken care of me during my heat, which I took as a sign that he was a good alpha.

I could feel his hot semen pumping into my womb, filling me with each pulse of his cock. The sensation was almost too much to bear, leaving me both overwhelmed and craving more.

"Does your pretty little ass need washing too?" Griffin playfully asked, his hands teasing my cheeks apart.

"Griffin!" I shouted when I felt his fingers explore my ass. I knew omegas were capable of getting knotted in the ass and that it brought the highest pleasure to be knotted there at the same time, but I was nervous as hell.

"Relax for me, honey," said Griffin. "Or is it too early for you?"

Closing my eyes, I started to feel the swirling of his fingers under the water as he played with my ass. My heart began to race as my breathing quickened.

"Don't stop," I gasped, feeling his fingers push deeper between my ass cheeks.

GRIFFIN'S FINGER suddenly slipped inside me, and I yelped just as the bathroom door swung open. I looked up to see Talon through my hazy fog of desire.

"Am I interrupting something?" Talon asked with a raised eyebrow, leaning against the doorframe. His gaze roamed over Griffin and me, taking in our intimate position.

"She's busy," Griffin said, a slight annoyance in his voice. He didn't remove his finger from me, continuing to tease and torment me even as we spoke to Talon.

"Relax, brother," Talon said, a smirk playing on his lips. "I just came to see how things were going. It's been a while since Carmen's last knot."

"Griffin already knotted me," I admitted, feeling vulnerable as I looked down at our connected bodies. My face flushed under Talon's intense gaze, knowing he wanted me for himself next.

Talon cleared his throat, his eyes dark with lust as he gazed at my exposed breasts in the soapy water.

"Well, I'm looking forward to knotting you soon," he said, lingering in his eye contact with me, causing my heart to race.

After he left the bathroom, Griffin captured my mouth in a passionate kiss, all the while wiggling his finger in my ass. I kissed him back with equal intensity, losing myself in his embrace as our tongues danced around each other. The sensation of being so thoroughly claimed by this alpha was intoxicating as I moaned against his lips.

Once Griffin's knot released me, he stood up in the tub, still carrying me. The sound of his wet feet echoed through the enormous white bathroom. Water dripped from our bodies, creating small puddles on the tiled floor. He grabbed a couple of towels hanging nearby and wrapped one gently around my back.

"Let's go, sweetheart," Griffin murmured, hoisting me into his arms. I held on tightly, still feeling weak with desire after he played with me endlessly in the tub.

We entered the bedroom to find Logan smoothing out brand new sheets on the bed. Talon was already there, watching me intently.

"We've changed out the mattress, too," Talon said eagerly, and I smiled at him. I still needed to know more about him, but I'd make it a point while we were cuddling and knotted together.

Griffin gently placed me on the bed with a wink, and I blushed while Talon kept his gaze on me. After Griffin moved aside, Talon walked over and lay next to me, wrapping an arm around my waist.

He pulled me close, and the warmth from his alpha body collided with my heated skin. Logan pressed himself against my back, his hands roaming down my spine and squeezing my ass cheeks.

"Going to get food for our omega," Griffin announced, making his way toward the door after throwing on a spare bathrobe from the closet.

My heart pounded at being called their omega, and something about it felt right, even amid my recent rejection.

"Are you ready for me?" Talon asked, and I nodded as he

kissed me on the mouth. His lips were firm and demanding against mine, reminding me of his alpha need. "Let me check your pussy."

Logan immediately lifted my leg, hoisting it over his bare, hairy thigh as Talon reached between my legs.

"Make sure she's wet," Logan instructed and then to me, "This is Talon's first time."

"Oh," I breathed as Talon's fingers made contact with my naked and exposed pussy. His fingers explored and hesitantly pushed into my hole, causing me to gasp.

"Oh fuck, am I hurting you?" he asked, removing his fingers.

"No, not at all," I breathed, enjoying this so much I thought I might faint. "Keep going... please."

It felt so freaking good to feel his finger swirling around inside of me.

"Okay, good," said Talon, kneeling between my thighs so he could inspect me further. He pushed his finger into my pussy again while rubbing my clit with his thumb. "Full of slick. That's a good sign. Your pussy is adorable and pink."

"Oh," I said, my heart pounding hard as he added another finger into my pussy.

We all heard the squelching sounds my pussy was making and my face heated with embarrassment. Being in heat required me to be as open as possible with alphas. Literally. And I wasn't ready for it.

"Might be time to fill her pussy," Logan suggested, his voice hoarse with lust as he watched us. I whimpered softly in agreement, craving relief from the pain of my heat.

"Spread for him like a good omega," Logan instructed as he guided me onto my back. Talon undid his pants, revealing his powerful, angry erection.

My breath hitched at the sight of his cock, eager for him to be inside me.

"Feel it," Talon said, and I wrapped my fingers around his throbbing length, the veins bulging beneath my touch. Slickness dripped from my core, anticipation mounting as Talon positioned himself in front of my clenching pussy.

"Please," I begged, feeling the pain from my heat rising to my belly. I was getting desperate for a thick alpha cock to fill the void within me.

He pushed into me slowly, his cock stretching me to accommodate his size.

My eyes rolled back in pleasure as he began to thrust.

"So tight, oh my fucking god," he groaned as he pressed himself deeper into me.

"Isn't she?" Logan whispered, watching me moaning on the bed and pinned down by his packmate. "Do you like it when he's deep inside you, honey?"

"Yes," I squeaked, my heart racing. I was shy, but I didn't think Logan praising me would turn me on so much.

"You look so beautiful getting fucked," Logan cooed as he circled my clit and sucked on my nipples. "Talon, make her boobs bounce for us."

Talon's thrusts became more powerful and more intense- nearly sending me over the edge, combined with Logan's fingers strumming my clit.

"Oh god," I moaned.

"Let it out, my best friend," said Logan. "My omega."

I shattered all over his fingers and around Talon's dick thrusting hard into me relentlessly. My pussy throbbed and clenched repeatedly until I was about to faint. But Talon's release came soon after, and he growled as he exploded into me.

Fiery, hot semen spurted straight inside of me, cooling the pain from my heat almost instantly. It was like my body knew that it needed to produce a baby for this pack and it was happy for now.

"You're huge," I gasped when Talon's dick swelled inside of me, holding my pussy captive for the next thirty minutes. He grinned, taking it as a compliment, and Logan chuckled behind me as he rubbed my ass.

"Did he do a good job for his first time? You took his virginity, Carmen," said Logan.

"Talon did amazing," I said, smiling as we looked into each other's eyes in the bed as I wiggled over his giant knot.

Talon chuckled softly. "I'm glad you enjoyed it because I sure did." His green eyes sparkled as he looked at me with affection.

My heart pounded, realizing the alphas could all fall in love with me. I wasn't ready for that, even though it sounded wonderful. My heat was really clouding my brain, so I needed to wait until it was over to make any long-term decisions about my life.

Logan began planting gentle kisses on my shoulders, his hands roaming down to play with my ass again.

"Your ass is so firm and amazing. Do you work out?" he murmured against my skin.

"Not really; I chase after kids all day at my job," I said, turned on by his nearness but also feeling weird since he was my best friend. This brought another layer of closeness between us, and it felt cozy in a way.

His touch reminded me of how Griffin had played with my anus in the bathtub earlier, and I felt a new wave of arousal wash over me. Hesitantly, I turned to look at Logan with a shy smile.

"Would you... um, do the same thing Griffin did to me?" I asked, my voice barely above a whisper.

I felt his smile against my heated shoulder from behind. "What did he do to you, baby?"

"Well, in the tub... he played with my ass," I said, wishing I hadn't said anything since he was asking me to elaborate.

"How? You need to be more specific, darling," said Logan, his question causing my pussy to clench around Talon's cock.

"Fuck," muttered Talon. His eyes rolled back from the pleasure of his first time, and I was glad that my pussy satisfied him.

"Umm, I want you to play with my asshole," I admitted, feeling embarrassed but also horny as hell. I wanted to feel the sensations back there again, as well as the electricity.

"I would love to," he crooned in my ear as he spread my ass cheeks apart. Suddenly, I felt his face between my cheeks and something wet pressing against my crack.

Oh hell, he was *licking* me.

But I kept quiet, my face red as a cherry as I looked over at Talon, who was watching me intensely.

"You're enjoying that," he said. "You like it when they play with your butt?"

Suddenly, I heard Logan sniffing my asshole, and I bit my lip shyly. "Yes, kind of."

"Don't be shy, baby," said Logan, my once best friend now furiously licking around my asshole. "Tell him how much you love it when I do this."

Suddenly, he pressed his tongue into my asshole, and I gasped as I felt my anus stretching. My slick coated the entrance, so it didn't hurt, but it still surprised me.

"What is he doing to you now?" asked Talon.

"He's umm... his tongue is inside me," I said, barely able to talk as I took in the odd but unique sensation of Logan's wriggling tongue in my ass.

Talon reached down and started to play with my clit, still sensitive from my last orgasm. Just at that moment, Griffin walked into the room carrying a steaming plate of food that made my stomach growl with hunger.

I looked up, mortified to be caught in this position—sandwiched between two alphas, Talon's knot still inside me while

Logan's tongue teased my anus. But I shouldn't be embarrassed, damn it. Alphas shared their omegas, and this was perfectly normal.

Griffin smiled warmly as if nothing was happening.

"I've brought food for our omega queen," he said, making me blush even harder as my pussy clenched around Talon's thick knot and Logan's fingers began to play with my asshole.

"I am hungry," I admitted, smelling the enticing aroma of chicken tenders and macaroni and cheese that filled the room.

"I will feed you, honey," said Griffin as he offered me a huge forkful of macaroni. The cheesy goodness melted on my tongue as I swallowed it quickly. "Ah, our omega is starving."

"Yes, feed her," barked Logan, stretching my ass with his fingers as he massaged my ass cheeks.

Griffin hurriedly pushed a second forkful of food into my mouth, and before I could swallow, the next bite hovered before me. *Wow, being an omega was pretty amazing, aside from all the heat pains.*

I nearly choked on the macaroni as Logan swirled his tongue into my ass, making me moan in pleasure. My pussy clenched again around Talon's dick as I started to feel slick seeping from my asshole.

"Very nice," said Logan, popping his tongue out. "Your slick is drenching the sheets, baby. Would you like for me to continue while you eat?"

"Yes," I gasped around another bite while Griffin now fed me with his bare fingers. His thick fingers pushed into my mouth, and I struggled to take in the mac n cheese.

"You need to lick my fingers, honey," said Griffin, and my heart pumped wildly as I hastened to obey while Logan increased the pressure against my asshole.

As I sucked off each of Griffin's thick fingers, he groaned, his eyes rolling back as he grabbed my hand to touch his hard cock. Horny again, I squeezed his bare cock up and down while Logan began pushing himself into my ass.

I could feel Logan's cock pressing against my anus, and my heart rate quickened. As I rubbed Griffin up and down, Logan stretched my ass with every inch of his dick. I gasped when he pushed inside of me all the way, stretching me fully.

"Ah, that's very nice," groaned Logan from behind, breathing heavily into my ear. "Do you like this best friend?"

"Yes, oh my god," I moaned as he took my ass like it would be the last time we would be together.

While Logan ravished my behind, I focused on Griffin's throbbing cock in my tight grip. It was thick and pulsating with desire that matched mine.

"Griff," I moaned his name as his strong hand enveloped mine, showing exactly the pressure he needed - combining our efforts on stroking his rock-hard erection. He groaned under his breath, a low guttural sound drowned by the heavy breathing of Logan behind me.

Logan drove into me again from behind, causing us all to jolt forward – intensifying every sensation tenfold.

"Damn...you're so fucking tight," said Logan, his hot breath grazing over my neck...his thrusts becoming deeper and more aggressive to claim my ass.

Slick spurted from my ass, and I gasped at the warm sensation as I squeezed around Logan's cock.

A muffled grunt erupted from Logan, promptly followed by another roar throughout the whole room.

"Fuck," he cursed, grinding against my asshole even harder before stilling completely. "Baby...I'm about to." Another short pause before finishing. "Knot"

As soon as he said those words, Griffin erupted into my hands, his sticky warmth released all over my lower belly in long, powerful spurts.

"Goddamn," said Talon watching me being taken while

still knotted to me. All three of us collapsed onto the bed, with Logan spooning me from behind and Griffin lying horizontally below my feet while massaging his knot.

"Fuck that was intense," said Logan, softly stroking my asscheeks. "Are you glad you didn't kick us out?"

"Logan," I groaned, not wanting to be reminded of the day's events.

"I'm just kidding, baby," he said, inhaling my hair. "We'll take good care of you during your heat."

chapter 15

. . .

Carmen

Two weeks later, I stood in the kitchen with Griffin, feeling the heat from the oven warming me as we prepared a homemade pizza together.

As he chopped the tomatoes and bell peppers, I couldn't help but watch his flexing arms under the white tank he wore.

"You look so good," I said, and he grunted in response. "And I didn't know you were such an expert with a knife."

A slight smirk played at the corner of his lips. "I'm an expert at many things, honey."

My heart raced as I imagined all the things those expert hands had done to me over the past few days when I was in heat. Warmth pooled between my thighs as I thought about my time with Logan and his pack. They had taken care of me so well during my heat, and I had gotten too comfortable with them.

It seemed too good to be true, but I wondered what would happen now that my heat was over. *Were they still interested in me?*

I sprinkled cheese generously over the sauce, trying to sort out my growing feelings for Griffin and the pack.

"Do you like having an omega around?" I asked.

"I'm loving it," said Griffin. "Because I love you."

My heart stopped as I paused with a handful of cheese between my fingers. I could hear the thunder of my heart pounding in my ears, and it made our connection feel a lot more real.

"I love you too," I said, knowing how I felt about him. He was one of the most attentive alphas I had ever met, playing a crucial role in mending my broken heart.

Griffin smiled, then glanced down at my hand. "That cheese is melted by now."

"Oh goodness," I said, throwing the glob in the trash and washing my hands, my heart still racing. When I turned back around, he had already taken care of the pizza and put it in the oven. He looked at me with love in his eyes, and I nearly swooned at the intensity of his gaze.

"Pizza should be done soon," he said.

"Have you always been this great of a cook?" I asked, trying to keep the conversation light to avoid getting knotted up again too soon.

"Growing up, I had to learn how to fend for myself," he replied as he washed his hands. "Cooking was one of the many skills I picked up."

"Well, it did come to good use," I said. His eyes met mine, and an electric current flowed between us.

"It did because I get to feed my omega," said Griffin.

"You feed me well," I said, letting out a soft giggle, and he kissed me on the lips right there. I savored every moment of his lips against mine. My heart swelled after confessing my love for him, something I had never thought was possible. "I can't wait to taste the pizza."

"Afterwards, I can't wait to taste you," said Griffin, biting and releasing my lower lip. We stood there for a while, hugging in the kitchen while the aroma of the baked pizza wafted around us.

"Cooking with you is fun," I said. "I used to dream of owning a bakery. Baking was my escape while living with my mom."

"She must be a piece of work," said Griffin.

"Just a little bit," I said. "Well, never mind, she is. She was critical about everything."

"What would she say if she knew you were mated to us?"

"That's actually a good question," I replied. "She always wanted me to be part of Henry's harem of omegas."

"Really?"

"Yeah," I said, hearing the shock in his voice. "My mom adores Henry and thinks he's the greatest gift on Earth. Anyway, I never opened the bakery, obviously. My babysitting business gives me joy."

Standing here and talking to Griffin was such a nice change from the physical connection and sex all the time. I mean, sex was great and all, but I needed to know who the hell I was going to commit to.

"You would make an amazing mother. I could feel it," Griffin said.

"I've always wanted to be one," I admitted, being vulnerable. "To be a mother."

"Maybe someday," he murmured, his voice low and seductive, causing butterflies to flutter in my belly.

⁂

AN HOUR LATER, I was sitting with Logan, Talon, and Griffin in the dining room, eating pizza for lunch. Glancing out the window, I noticed the snow falling heavily, blanketing the trees in a thick layer of cold, white fluff.

"So what's going to happen now?" I asked. "Obviously, we

can't go back to the Alpha Compound, and I don't want to live here in the snow forever, even though it's magical."

I gazed longingly outside, wishing I could escape to a place where the sun shone brightly, warming my skin and melting away the chill in my bones.

"Maybe we should think about moving somewhere warmer," Logan suggested, taking a hefty bite of his pizza slice. "Florida, perhaps?"

"Really?" My heart leaped at the idea.

"Anywhere you want to go, sweetheart," Talon said, winking at me.

"Yes, I love the idea," I said, imagining myself basking in the sun on a beach far away from this dreary place.

"Done," Griffin said, looking up from his phone. "I've booked flights for tomorrow morning."

"What?!" I shouted, but inside I was freaking out. We were really flying out of here tomorrow.

"Is that okay, Carmen, love?" Logan asked, smiling as he wiped his mouth with a napkin.

"I'm freaking excited," I said, unsure how they would manage to get us a place to live and handle all the logistics. But I knew Logan came from wealth, and he didn't look worried, so I shouldn't be either.

"We'll find a new home there. One where we can all be happy," Talon assured me.

"Oh wow," I whispered, feeling tears prick at the corners of my eyes. "You have no idea how much this means to me since I pretty much lost everything because of Henry."

"Anything for you, Carmen," Logan said, his voice low as he gazed at me. "We just want you to be happy."

My heart swelled with excitement as the reality of moving to Florida sank in. I couldn't help but imagine the life we would have there—the warm sun on my skin and the salty ocean breeze. Even though I had lived in the Alpha

Compound my entire life, we had books that helped me envision life outside of it.

"Where are we going to live?" I asked, already picturing us settling down in a cozy beach house while gathering around a bonfire to make s'mores.

"Somewhere near the coast," Logan replied, his eyes twinkling at my excitement. "I'm delighted that you chose to give me and my pack a chance. Seeing you happy makes it all worthwhile."

We finished our meal, chatting excitedly about the upcoming move and making plans for our new life together in a different state. But as I stood up to clear the dishes, a wave of nausea washed over me, and I gripped the edge of the counter for support.

"Excuse me," I mumbled, hurrying to the bathroom and barely making it before I bent over the toilet, retching violently.

As I wiped my mouth with the back of my hand, worry gnawed at the pit of my stomach. This wasn't the first time I had felt nauseous recently, but I had brushed it off, blaming it on the heat. Now, though, I couldn't ignore the unease that had settled in my gut.

Could I be pregnant? The thought made me giddy. I knew there was always a possibility, given my heat phase, which I shared with the alphas, but the idea of becoming a mother scared me a little, even though I thought I was prepared.

I took a deep breath to steady myself before stepping back into the kitchen. The alphas looked at me with concern, but I forced a smile because I wasn't sure yet.

"Everything okay?" Talon asked gently; his brow furrowed in worry.

"I'm fine," I assured the pack, trying to stay calm. "It's probably just the pizza. I'm going to start packing now."

"Alright, I'll take care of the dishes and join you," said

Talon, with the alphas agreeing as they ate more slices of the jumbo pizza.

Later that night, the nauseating sensation intensified, and before I knew it, I was hunched over the toilet, vomiting. A wave of embarrassment washed over me as I realized the alphas must have heard my retching.

"Carmen, you alright there?" Logan's concerned voice called through the bathroom door.

"Yes," I weakly muttered, but he wasn't convinced. Logan slipped into the bathroom and knelt beside me, sweeping my hair back from my face with a gentle hand as I tried to catch my breath.

"I'm here," he said, his sandalwood scent comforting me even as I continued to empty the contents of my stomach. His presence was grounding, a solid anchor during my physical discomfort.

Finally, the nausea subsided, but I was trembling afterward. Logan helped me stand, guiding me to the sink, where I rinsed my mouth out and quickly brushed.

"I don't know what happened," I said, swishing my mouth with water to get rid of the acidic taste.

"It's okay," said Logan, watching me silently as I dried my face with a hanging towel.

I hesitated, wondering if I should tell him about my suspicions. But when I looked into his eyes, all I saw was love. "I've been feeling nauseous lately, and my stomach feels weird. I don't know if it's just something I ate or... something else."

"Something else?" Logan prompted, leaning against the door.

Swallowing hard, I confessed, "I've been wondering if... maybe I'm pregnant."

He was quiet for a moment, which worried me, but then he smiled. "Wouldn't that be amazing?"

"You're not scared?" I asked. "We've only been together like this for a couple of weeks."

"But we've been close friends for years. I'm more than ready to love you," he said. "And the baby."

"I love you too," I said.

"Damn, it feels so good to hear you say that," Logan said, grinning. "My beautiful little omega."

He squeezed my ass, and I shook my head, giggling as we walked back into the bedroom, where there was a mess of suitcases and clothes on the ground from when the alphas had been packing.

"Is everything alright?" Griffin asked, and I could tell that he and Talon were anxiously waiting for an answer.

"Maybe," I hedged, not ready yet since I wasn't sure. "I think it was just something I ate. My stomach still feels a bit off, though."

But Logan quickly interrupted me, "Buy a pregnancy test for her. It's very early, but her scent is a little off."

"I'll buy one," said Talon, immediately throwing on a coat and his boots, his eyes glimmering with excitement. "I'll be back soon."

As I folded each item of my clothes, my mind whirled with excitement in case it was actually true. I waited eagerly for Talon to return, and it seemed like he was taking forever.

"You're excited," Griffin said, capturing my hand in his, and I turned to smile at him.

"It's finally my turn," I said. "Maybe."

"It will be," he said with certainty, just as Talon came through the front door. He hurried to the bedroom, and I smiled as he held out the pregnancy test for me.

"There you go, baby," said Talon. "Just know that we all love you no matter what happens."

"I love you too," I said, kissing him on the cheek before I hurried off to the bathroom. After peeing on the stick, I set it on the counter and washed my hands. "We just need to wait four more minutes."

"Damn, this is killing me," said Logan.

"Tell me about it," said Griffin. "This is worse than any wait I've ever felt."

I paced around the room, feeling more anxious than the three of them combined. When the alarm blared on my phone, I rushed to the bathroom and picked up the test.

Wait, what?

It said negative, and I reread it to make sure. I really thought... *forget what I thought*. I immediately threw it in the trash and held onto the counter for a minute.

"Carmen?"

I didn't want to tell the alphas the disappointing news. Maybe they would be relieved, but I felt a little shattered. Was there something wrong with me? I just went through a fucking heat, for god's sake.

Licking my lips, I walked back into the bedroom, shaking my head as tears streamed down my face.

"Aw, baby," said Griffin, rushing over to me. Logan and Talon joined in, hugging me tightly. I was grateful it wasn't just me feeling disappointed. "It was your first heat. I'm sure there's nothing to worry about. We'll try again."

"We'll put a baby in you," growled Logan. "Don't worry. During your next heat cycle—before and after—we'll knot you over and over until you're pregnant."

chapter 16

. . .

Tyler

"What's going on?" I asked Henry as I stood in his lavish chamber seven months after rejecting the omega I loved. My boots sank into the green velvet carpet as I waited.

He only summoned me to his personal quarters during an emergency, and to me, there wasn't one happening at the compound currently.

"Glad you could get here on time," Henry's smooth voice cut through my thoughts. He lounged casually in a luxurious armchair, wearing a plush robe.

"So what's going on?"

"Are you in a hurry to go somewhere, Tyler?"

I sighed. "Cut the crap, Henry. You're not going to intimidate me like your cronies."

Henry laughed, looking more excited than ever. "That's why I hired you, Tyler. Anyway, I've received news."

"News?"

"About Carmen," Henry said nonchalantly, making my heart clench painfully at the mention of her name. "She's living in Florida now with Logan, the traitor, and his pack."

"Are you sure?"

"Of course, I'm sure. And I'm not allowing more alphas and omegas to disappear from our home again. It will not be tolerated."

My mind raced with worry that he still hadn't gotten over his obsession with Carmen. My rejection of her had to be worth her safety, at least, but somehow he'd gotten intel on where she was.

"How did you find her?"

"I had people looking for her, and it seems she's living in a beach home... for now."

"What if she's already bonded to her pack?"

The thought of her permanently marked and bonded by Logan's pack made my stomach twist, but I had brought this punishment upon myself.

"I will still have her," Henry said. "I'll need to come up with a fitting punishment for Logan and his pack for stealing her from me. They will need to be set as an example for the entire community."

Fuck my life.

"It's not a good idea. You'll lose loyalty."

"And I've already lost it. What more can I lose?" Henry replied with a smile.

"Even if Carmen is already bonded, you can't just waltz in and mark her again," I said through gritted teeth, trying to make him see reason. "It could kill her, Henry. An omega needs to be marked by the same pack. Otherwise, they could die from disloyalty."

Henry's smug expression ignited a firestorm of rage within me. His callous disregard for Carmen's well-being made my blood boil, and I clenched my fists to keep from lunging at him.

"That will be the lesson that Logan and his pack will learn. Can you imagine his suffering once she's gone from his life?"

Henry said, smiling.

The air felt heavy and suffocating as I realized the magnitude of the situation. My breath came in shallow gasps, sweat breaking out on my forehead. I nodded in agreement, but internally, I knew there was no way in hell I would ever hand Carmen over to this monster on a silver platter.

"So what do you want me to do about it?"

"I'll give you her exact location, and you will bring her to me."

I thought about that for a moment. If I found her in time before Henry, there might be a chance to save her.

"That's fine," I said, sounding reluctant.

"Excellent," Henry's grin grew wider, his eyes gleaming with malicious satisfaction. "We make a great team, don't we?"

As I stormed out of the room, my mind raced with thoughts of Carmen—her radiant smile, the warmth of her touch, the intoxicating scent that clung to her skin. I couldn't bear the thought of her being subjected to Henry's twisted desires, and I vowed to do everything in my power to protect her.

I closed the door behind me, leaving Henry's oppressive presence behind. I needed to find Carmen, and fast. Time was running out, and failure was not an option.

"Keep it together, Tyler," I muttered under my breath, trying to shake off the crushing weight of fear and anxiety.

The sun had dipped below the horizon, casting a fiery orange glow over El Paso as I stepped out into the dry air. My heart raced with turmoil, torn between the weight of Henry's orders and my love for Carmen. I already felt sick thinking about how I had rejected her twice before, and now I was expected to carry out yet another betrayal, which I wasn't going to do.

She probably hated me, but I couldn't blame her. I had no idea how she would receive me now.

"Fuck you, Henry," I muttered under my breath, my knuckles white as I gripped my car door. I thought I had everything settled and perfect, but I had no idea that Henry was still lusting after Carmen.

I slid into the driver's seat and took a moment to steady myself. Taking a deep breath, I dialed Jaxon and Axel, my voice gruff with urgency. "Guys, meet me at the car. It's important."

"Alright, we're on our way," Jaxon replied. They were doing security rounds in Henry's mansion, where we primarily worked.

Within minutes, the car doors opened, and my packmates climbed into the vehicle, their expressions tense as they sensed my agitation. As we set off, I cast a sidelong glance at Jaxon, whose hazel eyes flashed with intensity, and Axel, whose icy blue gaze was sharp and calculating.

"Update us," said Jaxon.

"Listen up," I began, my voice strained. "We need to find Carmen. Henry's ordered us to bring her back."

Jaxon's brow furrowed, anger simmering within him. "Why the hell would he want her back?"

"Doesn't matter," I snapped, my grip tightening on the steering wheel.

"So you're going to do it?"

"No, we're going to warn her. I would never hand her over to him. What the fuck?"

"And if Henry finds out?" asked Axel. "He's fully expecting us to bring her back."

"We'll figure that out when we get there," I said, contemplating what I'd do after betraying Henry. I could never show my face again at the compound or see my family. Carmen hated me, so there was no chance of ever getting back with her. I was willing to risk my whole life in order to save her.

"We need to be smart about this. If Henry finds out we're

going against his orders, we won't be able to protect Carmen or ourselves," said Jaxon.

"Then we'll just have to make sure he doesn't find out," I replied, keeping my eyes locked on the road ahead.

As we sped through the streets heading to the airport - I couldn't shake the nagging feeling that whatever happened would change her life forever. But for Carmen, I was willing to face them head-on. I wouldn't let my love for her be overshadowed by fear of a tyrant. And if that meant defying Henry and risking everything, so be it.

chapter 17

· · ·

Carmen

My engorged belly floated like a balloon in the warm water as I lounged in the large bathtub, surrounded by Griffin and Talon. The weight of my seven-month pregnancy pressed down on me, making every movement an effort, but the bath made it easier.

"Can't wait for our baby to be born," Talon murmured, gently rubbing my swollen stomach. His fingers left trails of warmth across my sensitive skin. I smiled, remembering the moment I'd seen the positive pregnancy test, feeling a surge of love for the alphas and our unborn child.

"Same. I love you both," I whispered.

"We love you too, Carmen," Talon replied, his voice filled with tenderness as his hands began exploring my pussy underwater.

"Open up," Griffin said, drawing my attention. He held a grape between his fingers, smirking playfully as he waited for me. Parting my lips, I let my tongue glide over the smooth surface of the grape before slowly pulling it into my mouth, savoring its sweetness as I locked eyes with him.

As I chewed on the fruit, Griffin moved behind me, pressing his stiff cock between my ass cheeks.

"Ooh, what are you doing?" I whispered, my heart now pounding. My breath hitched in my throat when I felt Talon's fingers roughly stroking my pussy.

I choked on the grape, coughing lightly.

"Don't choke now, baby," said Griffin. "We know what you could choke on instead."

Quickly swallowing the grape, I tried to move away from the two probing alphas, but I was too large.

"This is getting out of hand. We were supposed to be having a relaxing bathtime," I whined.

"Isn't it always?" Griffin murmured in my ear, his hot breath soothing against my neck as he moved my long hair to the side.

"Didn't you just knot me before our bath?" I reminded him, my voice breathless. "You'll make me dirty again."

"Making you dirty again will be fun," Griffin growled, and I could feel his erection getting harder. "I didn't get enough of you."

"Well, I've had more than enough," I squeaked out when he squeezed my breasts.

"I can feel how ready you are, Carmen," Talon said gruffly. "Don't lie to us. You've been extra horny since you got pregnant, babe."

I gasped when his finger slipped inside me, making my heart thrum with anticipation. My body felt hotter and more flushed with their ministrations.

"Let's knot you one more time, Carmen," Griffin suggested, already lifting me out of the tub with Talon's help.

My heart raced, and a flush spread across my cheeks as water dripped all over the bathroom rugs. As he carried me in his arms, naked, our skin slipped and slid against each other with every step.

"Talon lay on the floor," Griffin said, setting me down on my feet. "Carmen, you're going to sit on his face. I need to see it."

"Oh my god," I said as Talon lay back on the floor. His eyes locked onto mine as I walked over to him.

It was awkward with my huge belly, but I straddled his head, feeling his warm breath against my slick folds, teasing me just enough to make me squirm.

As soon as his tongue darted out to taste me, I moaned when his sharp tongue flicked against my clit.

"So fucking good," he said, his voice muffled.

The three of us were dripping wet and glistening under the soft bathroom light. The cool tiles pressed against my heated knees as I rode his face with abandon.

Talon's tongue drove into my pussy, stretching me so nicely as I ground over his face while holding onto the edge of the tub.

The way his tongue swirled and flicked sent waves of pleasure coursing through me, my body releasing even more slick in response.

"Good girl," praised Griffin, but the sudden snap of a bottle opening caught my attention.

I glanced behind me to see Griffin pouring lube onto his hand. He approached me without hesitation, and my heart thundered in my chest when he spread my ass cheeks apart.

The slight chill of the lube contrasted sharply with the heat of my body straight from the bath.

I had let Griffin knot me in the ass several times before, but it still made me nervous. Despite my trepidation, though, there was something thrilling about submitting to him this way. I reminded myself to trust him, to trust that he would be gentle with me—at least until I wanted him to be rough.

"Lean forward, baby," Griffin instructed, and I bent over, feeling Talon's tongue delve deeper into my pussy. Talon gripped my wrists, steadying me as I presented myself to Griffin.

As Griffin began to tease my asshole with his lubed fingers, my nerves spiked, but the sensation sent a jolt of arousal straight to my pussy.

"Oh god," I groaned when he continued playing with my asshole. He suddenly squeezed my ass cheeks firmly, showing me that he was going to take my ass one way or the other.

"This is mine," Griffin growled, his breath hot against my ear as he rubbed circles around my sensitive asshole.

The sensation made my body go haywire, and I felt slick, drenching both my pussy and ass.

"Relax, baby," Griffin whispered, his fingers slowly easing into my tight entrance. The initial pressure felt uncomfortable, but as he gradually pushed in further, the sensation transformed into an exquisite combination of pleasure and pain.

"Oh," I gasped, getting nervous as I gripped Talon's upper arms. The stretching in my ass always felt new to me every time.

"Your little asshole got so fucking tight in the bath," Griffin purred. "But it's going to feel so good when I fill you up. For me and you both. Don't worry, little omega."

My heart raced with panic at the thought of him stretching me open even more, but I couldn't deny that I was getting hornier with each passing second. As Griffin continued to finger me, Talon squeezed my sensitive breasts to heighten the pleasure as he sucked on my throbbing hot pussy.

"Are you ready for me, baby?" Griffin asked. I nodded, biting my lip in anticipation.

With a gentle push, Griffin slid the tip of his dick into me. My body tensed as I adjusted to his size.

"So big," I muttered as he pushed himself inch by inch inside me, nibbling my neck. Finally sliding in all the way, I gasped when I realized he was fully inside.

"Fuck," he groaned with delight. "I'm going to thrust into your little ass now. Hold on, baby."

He gripped my waist as he pulled back, then thrust in. Talon's tongue pushed deeper inside my pussy, slurping up more of my juices.

Griffin pushed back into my ass, stretching me as my breathing quickened.

Talon's tongue worked magic on my pussy, pumping in and out like a machine. He was an alpha wolf, possessing a strength I didn't have. I moaned loudly, overwhelmed by the pleasure coursing through every nerve. Leaning forward, I reached down to grip Talon's hard cock.

His cock throbbed and pulsed underneath my fingers as I gripped him tight.

"Fuck, Carmen, you're so hot," Talon groaned, his voice muffled by my slick folds. I pumped his cock, feeling weak with desire yet determined to bring him as much pleasure as he was giving me.

I continued to rub Talon's cock while Griffin pounded into my ass. I couldn't hold it in anymore as Talon sucked on my pussy with renewed intensity.

My body reached its limit, and a shattering orgasm tore through me.

"Griffin... Talon... oh god!" I cried out, my voice echoing off the bathroom walls, knowing Logan was probably listening to us while he worked downstairs.

As I screamed in ecstasy, the world around me seemed to disappear. Talon's cock erupted, sending hot, white liquid splashing across my arms and chest.

Griffin growled, his orgasm flooding my ass with his warm seed. The sensation of him knotting me, combined with the slickness coating my insides, left me feeling sated and exhausted.

"Hot damn," Griffin panted. "I'll never get enough of your juicy ass."

As I slid off Talon's face, he looked up at me, his eyes filled with satiation. "You're absolutely amazing, love."

Flushed with pleasure and embarrassment, I couldn't help but blush at their words. When Griffin smacked my ass playfully, I let out a soft laugh, realizing just how messy we'd become.

"Time to wash you up again," Griffin said with a smirk, and together, they helped me back into the oversized bath.

LATER, after our impromptu second bath, I lay face down on the bed as Talon massaged lotion all over my body. His strong hands kneaded my muscles tenderly, easing any lingering soreness from our heated encounter on the bathroom floor.

"Logan must be working really hard," I said aloud. "He missed out on such a good time."

Talon chuckled as he continued to massage me. "Yeah, he's going to kick himself when he finds out what happened here tonight. Can't wait to cuddle with you."

"First, we'll have some hot chocolate," I suggested, already imagining curling up with my alphas, wrapped in their warmth and sinking my cold feet into theirs.

Griffin helped me off the bed as he sensually assisted me with my comfy cotton pajamas, constantly brushing against my breasts with a smile.

Talon went off to put on clothes while Griffin took care of me next.

"You're getting so big; it's perfect," he said, kissing my belly before covering it with my sweater.

"I'm glad you enjoy it," I replied, laughing as my pussy clenched with arousal again.

Wrapped in the soft, comfy cotton of my pajamas, I couldn't help but think about how hard it had been to find a pair big enough to accommodate my ever-growing belly. Pregnancy had its challenges, but finding clothes that fit comfortably was a battle all on its own. With a sigh, I tenderly rubbed my swollen stomach, feeling the life within me stir.

"Alright, little one," I whispered. "Let's feed you some hot chocolate."

I carefully made my way down the staircase, gripping the railing for support as I began my descent.

The comforting scents of cocoa and cinnamon wafted up from the kitchen, filling my soul with warmth. I looked forward to spending the evening cuddled up with my new pack, basking in the love of our little family.

But as I continued down the stairs, my steps faltered when I heard two voices in hushed conversation. One voice, I recognized as Logan's; the other, however, sent a shiver racing down my spine—it belonged to Tyler.

My heart pounded in my chest, and my blood ran cold as memories of his rejection flooded my mind. *What was he doing here? And why, now of all times, was he here?*

chapter 18

. . .

Carmen

The sound of Logan's deep voice mingled with Tyler's familiar timbre reached my ears as I slowly descended the stairs.

My heart raced, anxiety prickling through my body like a thousand needles. As I reached the bottom step, sure enough —Tyler was there, sitting among his pack members, engaged in conversation with Logan.

They looked up at me, their gazes locking onto mine.

"Tyler," I said, my voice barely above a whisper. "What are you doing here?"

He glanced down at my swollen belly, his eyes widening momentarily, but he said nothing. Anger surged within me, and I rounded on Logan instead, my hands shaking at my sides.

"Logan, why is he here?" I demanded, my voice rising an octave. "I'm done with him. I don't want to see him!"

Logan quickly rose from his chair, knowing how much seeing Tyler distressed me. He gently placed his hands on my shoulders, attempting to calm me down. "Tyler has some news he wants to share. It's important."

"And what news may that be?" I asked, sighing. My legs were getting tired, and I sank onto the couch next to Logan.

Reluctantly, I allowed myself to calm down. But my attention shifted back to Tyler as I glared at him, my hand protectively cradling my belly.

"Listen, Carmen," Tyler began, his voice strained with urgency as he took a step toward me. "Henry knows where you are, and he won't stop until he has you. He doesn't like to be slighted in the least, and I'm here to warn you."

My heart raced at the mention of Henry, and I tried to steady myself.

"Okay, thanks for the warning. You can leave now," I said, glancing away from him. I felt a strange mix of emotions with Tyler present. The wound in my heart still felt fresh, but I was determined to move on from him after everything that had happened.

"Wait," Tyler said, his eyes pleading with me. "I know full well that I don't deserve to be here right now in your presence, but you deserve an explanation."

"What explanation?" I said, holding back tears as I crossed my arms over my chest. "There's no way anything could explain the way you treated me."

"Please, just hear me out," he insisted, his gaze not leaving mine for a moment. "Do you remember the night I knotted you for the first time?"

The memory caused heat to rise in my cheeks, and I shifted uncomfortably. I wished I had just allowed Logan to knot me without Tyler being my first. I had given away my virginity to the last alpha on Earth that I wanted to be with.

"Yes, regretfully," I muttered. "But so what? What does that have to do with anything?"

"After I knotted you, I received a call from Henry," Tyler continued, his voice heavy with regret. "He demanded that I return and told me he was looking for you."

"Looking for me?" I asked, confused. "Why hasn't he moved on? I literally left the alpha compound and betrayed him."

"Because that's not how Henry operates," Tyler said, frustration seeping into his words. "You were never just another omega to him, Carmen. And he's not going to let you go without a fight."

"Are you fucking serious?" asked Griffin, handing me a cup of hot chocolate. I wasn't in the mood to relax anymore, so I set it down on the coffee table. "Don't worry, babe, we'll take care of him."

As I processed this new information, anger and fear warred within me. But one thing was certain—I couldn't let Henry find me, not now. I needed to protect my unborn child at all costs.

"Collecting omegas like trophies—that's what Henry does," Tyler explained, his voice filled with disgust. "I've seen it before. I had to stay away for your own protection, Carmen. I couldn't just hand you over to him."

"Oh really?" I asked, confused. "But what if we had stayed together? And I'm only asking hypothetically. Wouldn't he respect our relationship?"

"Respect?" Tyler laughed bitterly. "Henry doesn't respect the other alphas at all. He would've taken you in a heartbeat. That's why I asked Logan to take care of you, to keep you safe from him."

I suddenly felt the baby kick inside me. I looked down, one hand instinctively resting on my swollen belly.

"Leaving after raking my virginity was the worst thing you could do to me," I said, suddenly becoming emotional despite trying to hold it in. "You should never have done that if you weren't serious about me."

Before he could respond, a sudden alarm blared through the house. There was an intruder in the house.

"FUCK," said Logan, rushing to secure the front door.

The rest of us were frozen for a few moments, my heart pounding. Tyler's eyes went wide with alarm, and without hesitation, he rushed over to me.

He scooped me up into his arms.

"What are you doing?!" I yelled, punching his chest. "Was this your plan all along?"

But Tyler didn't answer as he rushed us to the back of the house and into the night air. He ran across the backyard and past the pool.

Oh my God, he was going to jump over the fence.

I shut my eyes tight while holding onto his arms. Tyler jumped over the backyard fence with me still in his arms, landing nimbly on his feet.

"It's Henry," he rumbled over the sound of my heart hammering in my ears. "We need to get out of here!"

But we were instantly surrounded.

Alphas clad in black—their faces hidden behind masks—encircled us like hungry wolves ready to pounce on their prey. Terror clawed at my chest as Tyler gently lowered me onto the ground, positioning himself between me and the enemy.

"Stay behind me, Carmen," he growled, his voice low and protective. I clutched my swollen belly, feeling the baby squirm inside me as if it, too, sensed the danger we were in.

"Leave," Tyler snarled at the approaching alphas. His fists clenched, ready for a fight. They didn't respond, but their threatening stances spoke volumes.

"Please, Tyler... be careful," I whispered, my voice trembling with fear for both him and the unborn child. He glanced back at me, determination etched into his eyes.

"I won't let them take you," he promised before lunging at the nearest attacker.

The sound of flesh meeting flesh echoed through the air as Tyler fought fiercely against Henry's cronies. Each one fell under his powerful blows, but there were just too many of them.

Eventually, they managed to overwhelm him, dragging him down onto the bloodied sidewalk. Panic surged through me as I watched them hold him, his face battered and bruised.

"Tyler!" I screamed, tears streaming down my cheeks.

The commotion behind me drew my gaze, and I saw Logan and the other members of Tyler's pack engaged in battle against more of Henry's men.

Suddenly, police sirens wailed in the distance. One of our human neighbors must have called. The clash of bodies and growls of pain filled my ears. My heart pounded wildly, and I knew I had to do something.

As I turned, two of the men grabbed me, hauling me toward a black van parked nearby.

"No! Let me go!" I shrieked, struggling against their iron grip. Desperation clawed at me, and I feared for both my life and the life of my child. "Help!"

Tyler started running toward me, and I screamed one last time before being shoved into the van. The door slammed shut, cutting me off from the outside world.

"Let her go!" Tyler's anguished shouts echoed in my ears as the van drove away from my alphas.

MY PULSE RACED as the van sped through the night, tires screeching in their haste to carry me further away from my pack. I could feel the cold floor beneath my feet, the unforgiving metal pressing against my bare skin. My heart sank deeper with every passing second like there was a crushing weight over me.

"Please," I whispered, choking back a sob. "Let me go. You don't have to do this."

A laugh echoed through the van, one of the masked alphas turning his attention to me.

"You think we have a choice, omega?" His voice was cruel and mocking. "We follow orders. You belong to Henry now."

"Like hell I do," I said, breathing hard. My hands balled into fists at my sides, though I knew it would be pointless to fight them all. But I refused to give up so easily. "I will never belong to him."

"Keep telling yourself that, sweetheart," another alpha sneered, his eyes raking over me hungrily. "Once he knots you, you'll forget all about your precious Tyler."

"Shut up!" I shouted, my voice breaking as tears pricked at the corners of my eyes. Desperation clawed at my chest, my mind racing with thoughts of escape, but the van was speeding down the highway.

"Leave her alone," one of the other alphas snapped, his tone surprisingly gentle compared to the others. "She's scared enough as it is."

"Aw, does someone have a soft spot for the omega?" The first alpha taunted, but the van fell silent after that, leaving me to stew in my fear and grief.

I banged on the tinted window, my fingers aching from the effort. The glass felt cold and unyielding beneath my palms, mocking my desperate attempts to escape. With a frustrated growl, I tugged at the door handle, but it remained steadfastly locked.

"Please," I whispered once more, my voice barely audible even to myself. "I'm begging you. Let me go. My alphas will pay you whatever you want."

Silence met my plea, the alphas seemingly unaffected by my pain. The only sounds were the hum of the engine and the occasional muffled curse as one of the alphas shifted uncomfortably in his seat.

I leaned back against my chair, trying to catch my breath. My heart continued its frantic pace, each beat a reminder of how dire my situation had become. The baby inside me stirred, and I placed a protective hand on my belly, vowing silently that I would do everything in my power to keep us both safe.

For now, all I could do was wait and pray that rescue would come before it was too late.

chapter 19

. . .

Logan

The scent of blood, sweat, and adrenaline filled the air as I grappled with one of Henry's men. Our wolf bodies collided, and my teeth bared in full rage.

They were threatening *my* omega. They weren't going to touch her.

My pack fought around me, their snarls mingling with the sounds of fists connecting with flesh.

In the midst of the chaos, the three wolves seemed to be listening to their pack leader telepathically. The wolf slipped from my grasp and bolted for the door, his pack members following suit. Their paws skidded on the hardwood floor, leaving trails of blood behind them.

I quickly shifted back.

"Come back here, you fucking cowards!" I shouted after them, but they were already gone. As I surveyed the living room, torn apart by the battle, a sickening realization washed over me.

Carmen was missing.

She had been there just moments ago with Tyler, but now, she was gone, and he was gone as well.

"Shit," I muttered under my breath, my heart sinking. We hadn't won the fight; they had captured Carmen and escaped. *How could I let this happen?* My chest tightened with guilt, anger, and a primal need to find her and bring her back to safety.

"Logan," Griffin called out, his voice strained from the fight, bloody claw marks visible on his chest. "What's going on?"

"Those bastards took her," I growled, breathing hard as my chest nearly exploded with rage.

"Fuck!" shouted Talon, slamming his fist into the wall. "We need to get back to the compound."

"Damn right, we do," I said, even though this meant waging war on Henry. We wouldn't rest until Carmen was back with us, safe and sound.

"Let's go then," Axel added, his torn clothes hanging loosely from his battered body. "We can't waste any more time."

I grabbed a fresh pair of jeans that weren't ripped before we bolted toward the van. Panic gnawed at me, realizing that Carmen was being taken straight to Henry. She didn't have much time. We spotted Jaxon and Axel holding a bloodied Tyler up between them as they made their way toward us.

"Listen, I don't have time," I barked at Tyler when he opened his mouth to speak.

"Logan, please listen to me," he rasped as he leaned against his comrades. "Let me join your pack."

"What makes you think I'm interested in that? What use do you bring except trouble?" I asked as I unlocked the van door and hopped into the driver's seat. I was about to slam the door in his face until...

"Henry plans on marking her as soon as he sees her," he shouted, and I paused reluctantly. "I can help you break into his home."

"You rejected her, left her vulnerable and alone. And now, because of your selfishness, she's in the hands of that monster," I growled, not easily swayed.

"Henry trusts me," said Tyler, wincing at my words. "I promise you we will get her back if it's the last thing I do on this earth."

Even if I wanted to fucking leave him there, I couldn't dismiss the fire in his eyes. He genuinely wanted to save her.

"What do you propose we do?"

"We need to combine packs so we can have a fighting chance against Henry."

A heavy weight settled in the pit of my stomach, realizing he was going to have a claim on Carmen, too, if he joined.

We needed him and all the information he had on Henry. I gritted my teeth, forcing down the bile that rose in my throat at the thought of relying on Tyler for anything.

"If you join, I'm your alpha," I reminded him, and his jaw tensed. "And if you so much as think about hurting her again, I swear to god, Tyler, I'll fucking kill you."

"Understood," he replied, his tone heavy with resolve. He bent his neck respectfully, even if it looked like it pained him. "I'm doing this for Carmen, and I won't let you down."

"Get in," I said, and Griffin slid the van door open for them. I shook my head, never imagining I'd have a pack of seven, including myself and our precious Carmen. "Let's go save our girl. We're going to bring her home, no matter what it takes."

"We need to get to the airport," suggested Talon calmly. "We'll get there before them and keep an eye when they bring her in."

"Copy that," I replied, gripping the steering wheel tighter as I pressed the gas pedal toward the nearest airport.

"Hey, Jax," Axel said. "You alright, man?"

"No, what do you think?" Jaxon snapped, his eyes never leaving the dark road ahead.

"Look, we need to stay calm," Tyler urged quietly. I knew that Jaxon always cared for Carmen, even when his ex-pack leader rejected her.

He obviously loved her, and I felt comforted by the knowledge that he would also do anything to protect her. His eyes were bloodshot, and his face was pained.

"Stay calm about what?" Jaxon shot back, fire blazing in his eyes. "Carmen's gone, and it's all because of you, Ty."

His anger was palpable, radiating off him in waves now that Tyler was his equal and no longer his leader. I needed to maintain peace within my pack, no matter the tension between them or how much I despised Tyler as well.

"We've got a plan," I barked at them, my voice strained as I fought to keep my emotions in check. "We're going to get her back, and you're going to be officially one of her mates. But we need to stay focused, Jax."

Jaxon exhaled sharply, but the tension in his shoulders eased ever so slightly.

"Yeah, alright," he muttered before falling silent once more.

As I sped down the highway, I couldn't help but wonder if Carmen was scared or if she was being tortured at this very moment. If anyone touched a hair on her head... so help me God.

***

AN HOUR LATER, we were on a plane after buying last-minute first-class tickets. I didn't care about the price; all I knew was that we needed to get to El Paso, no matter what.

"Once we're in there, I'm going straight for Henry," Griffin growled, his knuckles white from gripping the chair so tightly. "I'll tear him apart with my bare hands for what he's done to Carmen."

"Dude, chill," Talon said nervously, looking around to see if any of the flight attendants heard anything.

"Count me in," I replied, breathing hard with impatience as the plane took forever to take off. "That bastard won't know what hit him."

"A couple of you will focus on getting Carmen out," Tyler reminded us as he sat behind us with his pack. "The rest of us will deal with Henry and his men."

"Right," Griffin muttered, though the fire in his eyes didn't dim.

As the miles slipped away beneath us, my thoughts kept returning to Carmen—her laughter, her warmth, the way she looked at me with those mesmerizing eyes. Fear clawed at my insides at the thought of her in Henry's clutches, but I forced it down, channeling it into a fierce resolve to bring her back safely.

"Logan," Tyler's voice broke through my thoughts, and I reluctantly turned to look at him. "When we get there, I'll lead you to where they're most likely keeping her. But you need to be ready for anything—they'll be expecting us."

"Let them," I spat, my anger flaring anew. "They won't stand a chance against us protecting our omega."

"Don't let your emotions cloud your judgment, or it could cost us everything."

As we drew closer to our destination, I felt the weight of responsibility pressing down on me, along with the knowledge that the lives of my pack, Carmen, and our baby were in my hands.

chapter 20

. . .

Carmen

The darkness enveloped me as I slowly awoke, my body stiff from hours of uncomfortable sleep.

My heart pounded in my chest when I realized I was still in the van, captive to the alphas who had taken me. I blinked, trying to adjust my eyes to the pitch-black, but it was nearly impossible.

"Hey, sleepyhead," a gruff voice snickered as the van door slid open, revealing two alphas wearing all black. The dry air hit my face, and I knew immediately that I was back at the alpha compound. My heart pounded harder as one of the alphas licked his lips, leering at me. "Damn, I wish I could have you for myself."

"Stand down," the other alpha barked, grabbing my arm and helping me out of the van. "She's for Henry, and no one else is to touch her."

As I stepped out onto the sandy ground, my body ached, and the reality of my situation crashed down on me.

I couldn't believe I was back at the alpha compound, with Henry's mansion standing before me. Fear and anxiety clawed at my insides, threatening to consume me.

The alphas wasted no time whisking me through the night and into the mansion. I half expected to see Henry greeting us at the door, but no one was at the door at this time of night.

The two alphas led me into an elevator, and I didn't bother trying to fight them off. They were huge compared to me, and I wouldn't stand a chance. My mind raced as I watched the numbers in the elevator fly upward. I rubbed the sleep from my eyes as my heart raced. All I felt was dread at this moment and wondering how I would ever leave this nightmarish place.

We stopped on the fourth floor.

The doors opened, and they led me down a hallway. Still no Henry, thank goodness. Maybe he was sleeping, but the sun was starting to rise now.

"You will stay in this room," said one of the alphas, shoving me inside before locking the door from the outside. I rushed to twist the doorknob, but it was too late, and now I was trapped in here by myself.

I turned, taking in the simple room with a single bed in the center and a chair next to it.

My heart raced, and I could hear my pulse throbbing in the deafening silence of the room.

I sat in the chair, trying to calm down by taking a few deep breaths. I thought about everything that had led me to this point—Tyler showing up randomly after my bath with the alphas and then Henry's men breaking into the house.

"Why the hell is this happening?" I whispered to myself, fighting back tears.

There were no answers, only the suffocating darkness pressing in around me. My thoughts raced, desperately seeking some sort of escape or plan to get me out here. I knew that as long as I was here, my life and the life of my baby were in danger.

I paced the dimly lit room, calmly rubbing my belly to ease some of my stress.

The old-fashioned lamp on the nightstand cast eerie shadows on the walls, making me feel trapped in some sort of twisted nightmare. Desperation gnawed at the edges of my mind as I searched for any kind of escape—a window, a loose floorboard, anything. But the window had been bolted shut, and I couldn't help but think of the worst-case scenarios.

What if there was a fire? I'd be trapped here to die without anyone knowing.

The thought made the air around me feel thick and suffocating. I sank onto the rug, trying to take deep breaths to calm myself.

I need to stay strong, I reminded myself. *Logan will be coming to get me.*

After a few more deep breaths, I managed to push away the panic, at least for now. I crawled into bed and turned off the lamp, plunging the room into complete darkness. As I lay there, staring up at the ceiling, my thoughts raced about Henry and what he could want from me now that I was pregnant.

I WOKE to bright sunlight streaming into the room. Hearing shuffling and muttering in the corner, I instantly sat up, my heart pounding.

Two female betas were rummaging through the closet, pulling out several white dresses. I was confused to see them there with the door wide open.

"What's going on?" I croaked.

"We're going to dress you today. I'm Sherry," said the older woman with short gray hair, offering me a smile that seemed both friendly and strict.

"I don't need—"

"And this is Teagan," she gestured to the younger beta, who had her blond hair tied in a ponytail. Teagan was focused on a dress, examining it critically.

"No, too tiny," she muttered, and I rolled my eyes, all too aware of how much larger I'd become during the pregnancy.

I slowly hobbled off the bed, needing to take my chance. I quickly headed toward the door, but Teagan called out in alarm, "Stop!"

I ignored her and rushed out the door; however, two alpha guards appeared at the doorway, their imposing presence daring me to cross them. Realizing I was under tight security, I scowled and reluctantly made my way back into the room.

"Carmen," Sherry began scoldingly, trying to defuse the tension. "We're just here to help you get ready. Henry has certain expectations for his omegas, and we need to make sure you meet them."

"What the hell does Henry want with me?" I said, breathing hard and trying not to scream.

"There's a rutting ceremony," said Teagan, as if it were very typical. "So we have to get you ready."

"Well, that's not happening," I said, unwilling to submit to such a humiliating ritual. My mind raced with fear and indignation, wondering how the hell my perfect life had turned into this.

Where the hell was Logan? He should be here by now.

"I've prepared a bath for you. It'll help you relax before the ceremony," said Sherry.

"An amazing honor, especially for a pregnant omega like you," Teagan added smugly, casting a sidelong glance at my swollen belly.

"Excuse me?" I snapped, taking offense at her condescending tone. "First of all, don't ever talk about my pregnancy like it's something to be ashamed of. And secondly, I am not doing any 'rutting ceremony' with Henry."

A bath sounded relaxing right about now.

I stomped into the bathroom, stripped down, and slid into the bathtub. The warm water felt lukewarm after spending time arguing with Teagan, but as I sank into the bath, memories of my last bath with Griffin and Talon brought tears to my eyes.

I missed my alphas.

Their comforting hugs and kisses at night, our daily routines and laughter—the conversations we would have about the growing baby inside me.

After the bath, Teagan and Sherry dressed me in a giant white dress, making me feel like a marshmallow bride. Sherry fussed over my hair and makeup, chattering about how pretty I'd be as Henry's mate. With every second of their excited chatter, my heart sank further.

Of course, they had nothing to worry about. They weren't omegas.

"My makeup looks horrible," I said, glancing in the mirror and trying to stay there longer instead of facing Henry. The longer I sat in my simple little room, the better.

"It looks just fine," said Teagan.

chapter 21

. . .

Tyler

My heart pounded in my chest as we gazed at Henry's mansion, where I had worked for years. The morning sun cast an eerie glow over the white stone walls.

Carmen was inside, and guilt wracked through me at the thought of her fighting off Henry. If only I hadn't rejected her, she wouldn't have been taken right from under my nose.

"Alright," I said, trying to keep my voice steady. "I'm going in. I'll pretend everything's cool between me and Henry so I can check on Carmen."

Logan raised an eyebrow, his dark eyes smoldering with distrust. "You sure that's a good plan? What if his goons rat you out?"

"Trust me, Alpha," I replied, quickly putting on my security badge. "I'm the last person they have on their minds after their great capture of Carmen."

It felt strange to call him Alpha, but I knew I had to relinquish my role as alpha for Carmen's sake because of my mistake. I deserved every bit of punishment my way.

Logan seemed to understand, nodding reluctantly with narrowed eyes.

"Text me updates," he warned. "And don't do anything stupid."

"Got it," I assured him. We had developed a mutual respect to get along and save Carmen. Axel and Jaxon joined me as we approached the mansion.

"Let's do this," Jaxon said, glaring into the sun. Our whole pack was on edge with this rescue mission. It could end with all of us in prison and Carmen marked by Henry.

"Act normal, guys," I advised. "Jaxon, ease up. You look like you want to kill someone."

"Maybe I do," Jaxon muttered under his breath.

"Remember," I reminded them, "if Henry suspects anything, take Carmen and leave. I'll kill him."

I had taken on the role of destroying Henry. It was my fault that Carmen was here, and now I was going to protect her with my life if it came to that.

As we reached the mansion's entrance, I greeted the security guards by the white gate, doing my best to appear casual.

They let us through without a hitch, and I breathed a sigh of relief. So far, so good.

As we walked in, I wasn't prepared to see Carmen there. She looked absolutely stunning in a beautiful white dress, being ushered by a couple of beta servants.

She looked like an angel, and it tore me apart to see her here. Carmen's piercing green eyes met mine, and my heart stopped for a brief moment.

My instincts screamed at me to protect her, to pull her close and never let go, but I couldn't give myself away.

"Tyler, what are you doing here?" Her voice was cold and distant, making me wince internally. She had no idea I was her alpha now, that I had joined Logan's pack for her sake.

I turned away from her to the betas. "Henry wants Carmen kept safe. I'm taking her from here."

The beta servants exchanged confused glances, but they knew better than to question an alpha's orders. As I reached for Carmen's arm, she jerked it away with a glare that could have set me on fire.

"You're never touching me again in *any* way," she hissed, the disdain in her voice unmistakable. "You're nothing but a monster in cahoots with Henry."

"Let's take the elevator," I said, ignoring her hurtful words, but I needed to act normal around the servants.

"I knew it," she muttered under her breath as we both stepped into the elevator along with Axel and Jaxon. She refused to look at them as well.

Once the elevator doors closed, Jaxon immediately pressed a kiss to her lips. She squealed in shock, and I sighed in exasperation.

"Jaxon!" I exclaimed.

"I'm with Logan, what the fuck?" she screamed, wiping her lips.

Jaxon was about ready to spill the beans on everything until I stopped him with a look. Telling her that we were her mates at that moment would be a mistake, as we reached our floor.

My heart raced with each passing second, knowing that any slip-up could jeopardize not only our safety but also her trust in me. We stepped out of the elevator, and I unlocked my office door, guiding her inside without a word.

Jaxon followed us in, his eyes locked on Carmen with an intensity that suggested he wanted to rut her right away. He shut the door behind us and locked it, securing our temporary refuge.

"This is my office," I told Carmen, keeping my voice low and steady. "You're safe here. For now."

"Safe?" she asked, glaring at me as she took a seat in the chair behind my desk. "I don't really feel safe being in Henry's home and getting pampered for his omega rutting ceremony like a piece of meat."

"Carmen," I started, but she cut me off with a glare.

"Are you going to help me get out of this hellhole and back to my pack, or are you just going to hand me over to Henry?"

"Yes," I said firmly, meeting her glare head-on. "Yes, I'm going to help you. But there's something I need to tell you first."

"What?" she snapped.

I hesitated for a second, trying to find the right words. "First of all, you can trust me, Carmen."

"No," she said, looking down, but I caught the look of hurt in her eyes. "You haven't given me a reason to believe anything you say anymore."

My heart broke at her words. *I had failed her.*

Taking a deep breath, I knelt before her, feeling the weight of her distrust bearing down on me. My heart thumped hard in my chest, being so close to her again.

"This may be difficult for you to understand," I began gently, hoping not to scare her.

"Go ahead," she said, her voice void of any care left in the world for me.

I had disappointed her.

"Logan and I... we joined packs. For you," I said slowly as she lifted her face to look at me. "I'm...we're your alphas now, too, Carmen."

Disbelief was etched onto her beautiful face.

"You're lying," she whispered, her eyes searching mine for any hint of deception. She looked confused and fearful as she backed away from me in the rolling chair.

"I swear on my life, it's the truth," I said, tentatively

placing a hand on her knee. "I did this to protect you, Carmen. To keep you safe. Will you give me another chance?"

chapter 22

. . .

Carmen

My mind raced as I tried to process what Tyler had just told me.

He had joined the pack, making him my alpha. The very thought filled me with uncertainty about how to treat him, mixed with anger.

He had already hurt me twice, and now he held power over me.

"There's no way in hell," I muttered, staring at the carpet as tears welled in my eyes.

"Carmen," said Tyler, his fingers gently lifting my chin. "It's already done. I'll do everything in my power to get out of here—especially now that you're my omega."

My heart pounded even faster as I met his gaze, aware of the pack connection between us. It felt as if our souls were already connected as one, but I needed to resist the pull.

"Oh my god."

My body betrayed me, a slick wetness growing between my clenched thighs. I could feel it soaking through my clothes, and I knew every alpha in the room could smell my arousal.

I felt a blush spread across my cheeks, heat pooling in my face.

"Only when you're ready for me," Tyler said softly, but his words did nothing to calm me down.

My heart raced, and I could hardly breathe as I slowly stood up from the chair in a daze. This wasn't happening. The alpha who broke my heart.

"I'll never be ready for you," I said, rushing to the door. As I flung the door open, I found myself face-to-face with a smiling Henry.

What the hell? This nightmare was only getting worse.

"You look absolutely stunning, my dear," he said smoothly. Fear gripped me as I backed away from him. Jaxon, Axel, and Tyler immediately stood before me, blocking my path.

"Henry, we need to talk," Tyler said, his tone firm.

"Make it quick," Henry replied, his eyes never leaving mine. "My bride is eagerly waiting for me."

With that, they left me alone in the room, the door closing behind them as they chatted on the other side.

My heart was still racing after Tyler's revelation. He was officially mine now, and I had no reason to doubt the connection that had suddenly formed between us. No wonder Jaxon had kissed me in the elevator. It was all starting to make sense, and I was so confused.

TREMBLING, I sank back into the office chair, my heart heavy with fear.

The lingering scent of Tyler and his pack enveloped me, reminding me of the shocking news he had shared. If he somehow got me out of this situation and brought me back home, I would give him a chance.

A very small chance.

On impulse, I opened a random cabinet in the desk, searching for anything to occupy my mind and distract me from what was happening.

My eyes scanned letters addressed to someone, curiosity piquing as I wondered who Tyler had been corresponding with.

To my shock, I discovered they were addressed to me—letters never sent.

Dear Carmen,

I don't know where to start. No amount of apologizing is enough for what I did to you. I was starting as a new guard, and I had to push you away...

And another letter buried beneath that one.

Dearest Carmen,

Carmen, my love, I know you'll likely never read this, but I can't help but pour my heart out on paper. I've spent years regretting the decision I made that day—rejecting you for what I believed was your safety. You deserved so much more than the life I could offer you.

Then, a third letter.

Carmen,

I miss you. Every day, I find myself longing for your presence, your smile, and the sound of your laughter filling the air. Your absence leaves an emptiness within me that nothing else can fill. Do you still have the baseball I gave you back in tenth grade?

Please forgive me for causing you pain. If only I could turn back time and choose love over duty...

Yours forever,

Tyler

The words brought tears to my eyes, and my heart ached with the raw emotions in the letters. Despite all the years, it seemed Tyler had felt the pain of our broken bond.

He knew we were fated mates, but he had fought against it.

As these thoughts consumed me, the door swung open. Dread coursed through my veins, seeing Henry had come back alone.

My stomach sank with instant dread. *Where the hell did Tyler go? Wasn't he supposed to be busting me out of here?*

"Come now, omega," Henry said, taking my hand in his. "We have a lovely dinner planned for us."

I swallowed hard, thinking about the rutting that would inevitably follow. The mere thought sent shivers down my spine, filling me with dread and despair.

MY HEART HAMMERED in my chest as I followed Henry to the elevator. The cold, metallic walls seemed to close in on me with him there.

"Ah, Carmen, you've been quite the elusive omega," he said, grinning as he held my hand tightly.

"Where's Tyler?" I asked, sweat pouring down the back of my neck.

"Tyler has a job to do," Henry replied dismissively. "He shouldn't have wasted time chatting with you."

"But why am I here?" I asked, trying to act as clueless as possible. Maybe I was here for a different reason besides being in his harem. *Why would he want me?* A pregnant omega who was literally about to give birth.

"It's simple, my dear. You're going to be my new omega," he answered with a grin, holding my hand to his heart. I tried to pull my hand away, but he tightened his grip.

"But I'm pregnant," I said. "I have a pack who loves me."

"They took you from me when they saw that I had an interest in you," said Henry darkly. "If they try that again, they will all be executed. No one will touch you after I mark you tonight."

Mark me? What the actual fuck? That was some serious commitment that happened if a pack vowed to keep their omega forever.

The elevator came to a stop, and we walked to the dining room—a beautiful space decorated with shimmering crystals that reflected the ambient light.

My heart continued its relentless pounding; I could hardly hear anything Henry was saying. All I could think about was how to escape this nightmare.

As we sat down, servants brought out platters of food—steak, broccoli, and potatoes. My appetite had vanished, and it felt like a knot had formed in my throat.

"Is something wrong, Carmen? You're not eating," Henry prodded, concern feigned in his voice.

"Um, just not very hungry," I mumbled, forcing myself to take a small bite, hoping to prolong our meal and delay the impending rutting. I wondered where the hell Tyler was.

Did he really leave after Henry's threat? I suddenly felt very alone and small at the table as tears ran down my face. None of my alphas had come to save me.

The only person who could save me now was myself.

A servant approached to pour more lemonade for Henry. Staring at my steak knife, I suddenly saw my opportunity and ducked under the table with it.

The cold metal pressed against my skin as I slid it into my bra beneath my dress.

I re-emerged from underneath the table, and Henry raised an eyebrow. "Everything okay?"

"Y-yes," I stammered, trying to sound nonchalant. My breathing was labored, and I was scared he could tell, but he seemed focused only on our impending union. "Sorry, I thought I dropped a piece of meat."

"Please, don't worry about that," he reassured me. "The servants will clean up any mess. You're going to be my wife very soon. You will be omega royalty."

As we continued our meal, my thoughts raced on how I would stab him. It wasn't the right time with all the servants watching. Maybe once we were alone.

The clink of silverware against my barely touched plate echoed in the tense silence as Henry took my hand, his grip firm and unyielding.

I froze, my heart pounding like a trapped bird against my chest.

"Time for us to get better acquainted," he said with an unsettling grin, excitement shining in his cold eyes. "It's a real ceremony. Several members of my pack will witness me rutting you."

I swallowed hard as we walked down a long hallway. Fear clawed at my insides as we approached a huge bedroom adorned with a gigantic white bed in the middle, covered in red petals.

The room was crowded with six stuffy alphas wearing suits.

Immediate fear consumed me as Henry closed the door softly behind us. "Men, meet Carmen. We will be sharing her tonight, after I've had my fill, of course."

"She's pretty. Very plump," said one of the alphas, admiringly.

"I have a pack," I cried out, crossing my arms over my chest to hide any evidence of the knife buried between my breasts.

"Isn't she?" Henry said, beaming. "We will all mark her after the rutting ceremony, and she will become the newest addition to our omega nest."

My heart thundered in my chest as I tried to back away, but Henry looped his fingers through mine, leading me toward the bed.

chapter 23

. . .

Logan

The heat of the sun bore down on me as I waited, hidden in the shadows outside Henry's mansion. My heart raced with anticipation and worry; my hands clenched tightly into fists. The sandy courtyard stretched before me, and all I could think about was Carmen.

I needed to know where she was and if she was safe.

After a whole hour, Tyler and his pack emerged from the mansion. Their faces were void of emotion as I watched them closely, trying to discern any signs of what had transpired within those walls.

"Where the hell is Carmen?" I muttered to my pack, unable to keep the concern from my voice. "Why isn't she with them?"

Tyler, Axel, and Jaxon made their way around the wall where we were.

"This fucking sucks," said Tyler.

"What does? Is Carmen alright? Where is she?" I demanded, fighting to keep my voice steady. My love for her was a storm raging inside me, and if I didn't get answers soon, I was ready to kill someone.

Tyler's face grew serious as he met my gaze. "I saw her. They're eating right now, but once they're done... Henry intends to rut and mark Carmen."

My eyes widened in horror at the thought.

I hadn't marked Carmen yet, and if Henry did it first, she would be forever bound to him. The engagement ring I bought for her felt like a heavy weight in my pocket, a symbol of my failure to protect her.

"Why aren't you with her?" I barked.

"I wanted to get backup before blowing my cover," explained Tyler.

"Once he marks her, she'll be gone forever," I growled. Tyler simply nodded, confirming my worst fears.

"Then what the hell do we do?" Griffin's voice cut through the tension like a knife.

"You'll go in as my prisoners. It'll get us inside," suggested Tyler.

I nodded in agreement. It wasn't ideal, but it was our best option. "Then what?"

"Once we're in, we find the room where Henry plans to claim her," Tyler said, his voice hardening. My hackles rose at the thought of another alpha rutting Carmen, let alone someone as vile as Henry.

"Alright," I ground out, clenching my fists. "I want to kill him."

"Leave Henry for me," growled Tyler, and I nodded. The only person I cared about was Carmen. "The rest of you should focus on taking down the guards and any other alphas that stand in our way."

"This is an all-out war," said Axel, puffing out his chest.

"I'm fucking ready," said Talon. "Every minute counts."

"NICE CATCH, TYLER," one of the guards sneered as Tyler led me into the mansion, handcuffs biting into my wrists. I burned with rage but kept my expression carefully neutral, playing the part of a defeated captive.

"Thanks," Tyler replied without missing a beat, his tone casual, betraying no hint of our plan to kill Henry. Beside me, Griffin and Talon were being escorted by Jaxon and Axel.

Disbelief washed over me as we entered the mansion despite the circumstances. We were finally in, and now we could move forward with our plan to save Carmen.

Tyler led us to his office, and once the door closed behind us, he swiftly removed my handcuffs. I rubbed my wrists, glancing around the room. "This is your spot?"

"Yep," he confirmed, already scanning the security monitors. He checked every camera, not finding Henry anywhere. "This room. This is where he is."

I looked at the screen, and all I saw was a closed door.

"Are you sure she's in there?"

"That's where he takes all his new omegas. They're definitely in there," confirmed Tyler, his jaw tense. I nodded, my heart pounding in my chest as we prepared to decimate some alphas.

chapter 24

My heart raced as Henry took my hand, leading me toward the bed.

His beady eyes flicked to the other alphas in the room, smirking as if he had just won a prize. I swallowed hard, knowing that my life would be completely destroyed in minutes.

"Get on the bed," he ordered.

"And if I don't?" I asked, keeping my voice steady.

"Depends if you like being manhandled," he replied, his gaze darkening as he leaned in closer. I immediately noticed the bulge in his pants growing more prominent.

My stomach churned with fear; he was unpredictable.

When I realized I had no other options, I cautiously climbed onto the bed, mindful of my pregnant belly. The scents of the alphas around me were intoxicating, causing my body to react, even against my will.

"She smells so fucking good," growled one of the alphas.

"Get on your knees," Henry demanded, and I complied, feeling the white dress fan out over the white blankets beneath me.

The sound of his belt hitting the floor and the clink of the metal buckle made my heart pound in my chest. My breasts felt heavy from pregnancy, swinging slightly as I moved into position.

"I'm pregnant, and I love my pack," I pleaded with him. "You're going to ruin my life forever."

Henry just chuckled darkly, clearly enjoying the sense of power he held over me.

I shut my eyes tight, my heart racing.

Fear consumed me as I tried to focus on the small steak knife tucked into my bra from dinner earlier. *How on earth was I going to stab Henry with it?*

Henry climbed onto the bed and positioned himself behind me, his hands beginning to lift my dress slowly, exposing my skin inch by inch. My breathing grew heavy and erratic. Each inhale was a desperate attempt to calm myself.

I needed to find the right moment.

My cheeks burned with embarrassment as my ass became exposed under the predatory gazes of the alphas around us. Their ragged breaths deepened, and I could sense their desire. I glanced back to see Henry's cock swinging behind me, his arousal clear.

With all the alphas distracted by my exposed ass, I decided this was my chance.

I slowly dipped my hand into my cleavage, pretending to undress further.

Instead, I clutched the knife handle, preparing myself for what I needed to do for myself and the baby. In one swift motion, I spun around, aimed to stab directly at Henry's heart.

But he was faster than I anticipated.

His grip on my wrist was quick, like a vice. Panic surged through me as I futilely tried to pull free.

"Feisty little thing, aren't you?" he taunted, his eyes wild with excitement. "I knew you'd try this."

"How?" I gasped, trying to buy some time.

"You think I didn't see you stash away your little knife? Ah, omega, when you put up a fight like this—it only makes me want you more."

The other alphas chuckled darkly, their erections on display as they watched me struggle to pull away from Henry's grip. He finally released me, but now he held the knife in his hand.

He pressed the knife to my throat with a grim smile. With the cold steel against my skin, I could hardly breathe from fear.

Henry's grip was unyielding as he slid the blade down my neck and traced it along my cleavage.

"Did you really think I'd be that dumb, sweetheart?" he sneered. "You must have quite an imagination to believe you could kill the leader of all alphas."

"Please," I begged, the quiver in my voice betraying my fear. "You don't need me. Find another omega."

He chuckled darkly.

"The moment I stepped into your little apartment and smelled your scent, I knew I had to have you. No other omega will satisfy me. Believe me, I tried."

"I'm not going to satisfy you," I cried out. "I'm not the one for you."

"Tell me, Carmen," Henry whispered, his breath hot against my ear, "do you want to live?"

I nodded, my heart pounding in my chest.

"Then relax and enjoy every minute of me," he purred, setting the knife aside. "Any other omega would die to be here rutted by me."

Suddenly, the door burst open, and a loud alpha bark reverberated through the room.

My heart soared when I saw Tyler, his muscular wolf form

dominating the space, rushing straight for Henry. I recognized him immediately by his scent, which was stronger in wolf form, and the dark color of his fur.

"What the fuck?" shouted Henry as Tyler dragged him off the bed by his teeth.

Before Henry's men could come to his aid, Logan, Axel, and Griffin lunged at the other alphas.

I watched in shock as Henry kicked and screamed, struggling in vain to free himself from Tyler's grasp. Overwhelmed by the chaos, I clutched my pregnant belly protectively, my heart racing.

As Henry shifted into his wolf form, he and Tyler snarled and snapped at each other, their anger palpable in the air.

The room erupted into a cacophony of snarls, growls, and the shattering of glass as the two wolf packs clashed in a brutal free-for-all.

I watched with a mix of awe and terror as massive wolves lunged, bit, and tore at each other, their powerful bodies crashing through the ornate furniture that had once adorned Henry's luxurious mansion. The scent of blood hung heavy in the air, mingling with the primal musk of anger and rage.

"Shit, Carmen, we need to get you out of here!" Jaxon's voice cut through the chaos as he shifted back into his alpha form and rushed to my side. His hazel eyes were filled with concern, his protective instincts taking over.

"We can't leave them," I protested, my heart aching for Logan, who risked everything to save me. But Jaxon was already lifting me into his arms, my frame feeling even more delicate against his muscular chest. "Jaxon, please..."

"We'll regroup, but right now, your safety is our priority," he said, firmly carrying me in his arms away from the chaos unfolding in the room.

I looked back one last time, searching for Logan and the rest.

My breath caught when I saw them squaring off against Henry, their feral snarls echoing through the space. Blood dripped from Tyler's shoulder, staining the white carpet.

Tyler glanced back at me, only to be bitten on the neck by Henry when he was distracted.

"No!" I screamed. Even though I didn't like Tyler, I didn't want him to die because of me.

"We need to leave," Jaxon grunted, rushing toward the door.

"Please let them be okay," I whispered, my grip on Jaxon tightening as we sprinted down the hallway, away from the violence.

"Tyler and Logan are strong. Don't cry, hun," Jaxon reassured me, his voice filled with determination to save me. My chest tightened with fear as tears streamed down my face.

"But what if they don't make it?" I said, my heart pounding. My worst fear of losing my entire pack washed over me. I would raise this baby alone with Jaxon. But if Henry survived, he would go after Jaxon next.

And I would be left vulnerable.

"They'll make it, I promise," Jaxon said, his voice unwavering.

As we fled Henry's mansion, the sounds of snarls and shattered glass faded behind us. All I could cling to were Jaxon's words, but I couldn't shake the sinking feeling inside me.

chapter 25

· · ·

Carmen

The rest of the Alpha Compound was alive with chaos as people were alerted to what was happening. The clamor of the crowd rang in my ears as Jaxon carried me through the commotion. Werewolves and guards loyal to Henry rushed past us, their expressions a mix of shock and urgency at the audacity of the attack.

They didn't even glance our way as they hurried into the mansion to save their leader.

"Oh my god," I gasped, my chest heaving with each breath. Fear constricted my heart as tears streamed down my cheeks. My alphas weren't safe at all right now. "We need to go back! Logan and the pack..."

"They can take care of themselves," Jaxon replied gruffly, his hazel eyes meeting mine for a moment before turning back to the path ahead. His naked body moved fluidly, muscles rippling beneath his tattoo-covered skin as he sprinted down the street—a familiar sight for an alpha after shifting.

"This is so horrible," I cried, panic rising within me at the number of loyalists supporting Henry.

"Helping you is my priority right now," Jaxon said tersely,

his jaw set. His silence about the situation infuriated me, but there was something in the depths of his eyes that revealed his own fear.

"Where the hell are we going to go now?" I asked. The only refuge I could think of was my small apartment or my mother's home.

"You will stay at our pack house," Jaxon replied, continuing to run through the streets as if carrying a heavily pregnant omega didn't faze him.

Taking deep breaths, I watched the streets blur by while people raised the alarm. A large group of werewolves brandished a black and red flag—one that wasn't Henry's. They rushed toward Henry's mansion, shouting about his downfall.

Hope surged in my heart that Logan and the pack would at least have some backup.

Jaxon continued running without pause until we finally reached a quiet street lined with sizable pack houses.

As Jaxon carried me through the gated entrance of a grand estate, I couldn't help but stare at the two life-sized ostrich sculptures that flanked the front door.

The sprawling white mansion loomed before us, illuminated by soft golden lights that framed its ornate architecture. A marble fountain featuring a howling wolf dominated the center of the circular driveway, surrounded by meticulously manicured gardens.

"Is this the house?" I asked, my anxiety still lingering at the edges of my mind. "It's beautiful."

Jaxon shifted me in his arms, glancing down at me. "Yes."

My heart clenched, and I bit my lip. I remembered Tyler's claim that he was my alpha now. Jaxon quickly opened the door using a code and locked it behind us.

As we entered the house, I caught glimpses of the opulent interior—gleaming polished floors, high ceilings adorned with elaborate chandeliers, and priceless works of art lining the walls. But I couldn't focus on the beauty around me; my thoughts were consumed with worry for the pack.

Jaxon deposited me onto the couch, then went onto grab two glasses of water for us.

My thoughts were all over the place.

Everything was moving too fast, and my pack was in danger. Jaxon tried to soothe me when he noticed that I wasn't relaxing against the couch.

"There's no use in worrying right now," he said gently. "You need to rest. All this stress isn't good for the baby."

"I can't relax right now," I whispered, taking deep breaths as I sipped the cold water. Jaxon watched me with concern as he rubbed my back.

"Maybe taking you to your nest will help calm you," he suggested as I numbly set the glass down. Nothing would calm me at this moment.

"It doesn't matter," I said listlessly.

Jaxon lifted me once more, carrying me up the tall staircase.

"Don't give up hope," he said, walking down the hallway with me in his arms. "They're still alive. I can feel it."

"Oh," I replied, the sinking feeling in my stomach easing slightly. "Could you feel it if something happened to them?"

"Yes, I feel the pain of our pack or any strong emotions they have. You will, too, once we mark you, babe."

As he set me down in a plush blue nest filled with soft cushions and velvety pillows, I sank into its luxurious embrace, surprised by how comfortable it felt against my stressed muscles.

"Interesting," I murmured.

"I will let you know immediately if anything happens," Jaxon reassured me, massaging my tense shoulders. "But for now, they're all okay."

It also reminded me that Jaxon was my alpha now.

"Why did Tyler join the pack?" I asked, desperate for any information that might make sense of my swirling emotions. "Was it forced or something?"

Jaxon hesitated, his hands stilling on my shoulders.

"Tyler felt guilty as hell for leaving you," he confessed. "He was the only one who knew how to get into Henry's place, and Logan figured a bigger pack would have a better chance of success."

"It's going to be really hard for me to forgive him for the way he ended things," I said slowly. "I really don't think I can get over it."

"Tyler is your alpha now," Jaxon whispered, and my stomach clenched. I didn't know if it was from fear or arousal.

"And you're mine now, too," I said, giving him a small smile. "That's the best thing that came out of this whole 'joining of forces'."

"Do you really think so?"

"I do."

As much as I wanted to deny it, part of me knew that Tyler and his pack would always hold some power over my heart—no matter how hard I tried to resist.

THE DARKNESS of the room wrapped around us like a cocoon for the next few minutes. Jaxon's muscular body pressed against my back as he sat behind me.

His strong arms encircled me, and I could feel the heat radiating from his skin, calming my frazzled nerves even as it stirred something else deep within me.

"Can't believe I missed it all," Jaxon murmured, his voice rough with regret as his hands, which had been massaging my shoulders, slowly slid down my arms and then across my pregnant belly. "The day you found out you were expecting... all those months after."

I swallowed, my heart aching at the raw emotion in his words.

"It's okay," I whispered, trying to reassure him that I had no hard feelings. "I know you had to follow Tyler's orders."

"Doesn't make it any easier," he admitted, his breath warm against my ear as his hand continued its journey, slipping down my belly and between my legs. The moment his palm cupped my pussy, my breathing hitched. My arousal ignited within me.

"Jaxon," I gasped, unable to suppress my moans.

"I missed you so fucking much, Carmen," he whispered as I relaxed against him, tilting my head to one side. He took advantage of the exposed skin, his lips attacking my neck with a ferocity that left me breathless. Jaxon nibbled and sucked on my skin, kissing every inch of my neck. "I want to mark you."

My breathing grew harder, and my heart raced wildly. "I want it too."

Then, without warning, he bit me. The pain was sharp and unforgiving.

Suddenly, tendrils of heat swirled around my belly and down to my pussy, our permanent connection forming with an intensity that left me panting.

"Oh my god," I whispered as my breasts heaved from arousal.

"You're mine now, forever," Jaxon growled, his tone equal parts possessive and tender. "Henry will never lay his hands on you again, if it's the last thing I do."

Desire coursed through me at his words, the fire from his mark flowing through my entire being. Jaxon gently kissed and licked the tender spot on my neck to calm the burn.

He hugged me from behind, and my entire body trembled with anticipation. I wanted him.

I could feel the dampness between my thighs growing as he continued to tease me, his hands lifting my white dress until it bunched around my hips.

His fingers gently traced my naked pussy lips until more slick bubbled out. Then he inserted a finger inside my channel.

"God, you're so fucking wet, Carmen," he growled thickly. He removed his finger from my pussy, a stream of sticky slick following. "Do you want a big alpha to take care of you, honey?"

"Mhm, I missed you too," I gasped for air, leaning back against him, weak. "I need you."

"What do you need, honey?" He asked, pushing two fingers inside my pussy, stretching me as he kissed my neck.

"I need your big knot," I whispered, as if a crowd of people were listening to us. But it was just us in this dark room, cuddled in my new nest.

"You drive me crazy, omega," he said, moving until he was in front of me. Then he took my hand and rested it over his massive cock. "Do you feel what you do to me?"

I could feel the heat radiating from him, the throbbing pulse of his arousal. I licked my lips in surprise, remembering the sight of him running naked through the streets earlier.

"Jaxon, were you this hard out there?" I asked, my voice breathy and teasing.

"Only for you, honey," he replied, his voice husky. "Forever with you."

I blushed at his response as I squeezed his massive cock in my hands. "I love that you're hard for me."

"Lay back and spread yourself for me," he grunted, and my breathing quickened as he helped me lie on my back on the cushions. "Open your legs, honey."

At his urging, I opened my legs wider, my pulse racing and my palms growing clammy as I surrendered myself to him.

He leaned down, pressing tender kisses onto my swollen belly, his warm breath making me shiver.

"Oh my," I breathed, craving more of him and gripping his forearms tightly. "Please, Jax, I need you inside me."

Just as I thought I couldn't take anymore, I felt the pressure of his hardness against my entrance.

He slowly pushed inside me, the sensation of being filled by him sending a rush of tingles all over my body. Our moans mingled together as he began to thrust, the room filling with the sounds of our skin against skin and heavy breathing.

I savored each thrust of his cock into me.

"Jaxon, I missed you so much," I cried out, my pussy stretching deliciously around him with each powerful stroke.

"Fuck, I missed you more," he growled, his cock pumping furiously into me, the thrusts bringing me closer to ecstasy.

But just as we neared the peak, his cell phone rang, the shrill tone slicing through the passion-filled air. He paused mid-thrust, snarling as he grabbed his phone from the floor.

MY PUSSY CLENCHED and throbbed around his warm cock while I waited impatiently beneath him.

Jaxon's eyes never left mine as he pressed the phone to his ear, answering gruffly, "What's going on?"

I tried to keep my breathing under control, not wanting whoever was on the other line to hear what we were doing.

"Are you really banging Carmen right now?" Tyler's voice came through loud and clear, making me blush furiously. Jaxon smirked at me, unfazed by the question.

"Fuck yeah, I am. Now, get on with it. Did you all make it okay?" he growled, maintaining eye contact with me the entire time as he slowly thrust in and out of me while squeezing my breast with his other hand.

"Yeah, he's dead."

"Fuck yes," said Jaxon, hanging up the phone and immediately continuing to thrust into me with even more energy than before. "No one's stopping me from knotting you tonight, honey. I love you."

His final pump sent me over the edge, my scream mingling with his growl.

"I love you too," I screamed as my orgasm took over my entire body, making me tremble and shake. His cock began to swell rapidly, knotting me to him. My climax, combined with the sensation of his cock swelling inside me, intensified the pleasure coursing through me.

We lay there, panting heavily, our bodies shining with sweat. Jaxon cuddled me from the side, pulling me against him while gently rubbing my back.

"I can't believe we had sex while the pack was fighting for their lives," I said, suddenly feeling guilty for losing control like this.

"They're okay," he reassured me. "Just like I said they would be. We did our duty as alpha and omega."

"So is it my role to just lie down on command and get bred?" I asked playfully, glaring at him with a mischievous twinkle in my eyes.

"Hmm," he started, a twinkle in his eye indicating he wasn't opposed to the idea. "It's called making love to our queen. You are our queen, and you will get knotted whenever you need it—to carry our babies."

chapter 26

. . .

Carmen

An hour later, as I lay entangled with Jaxon in our nest, the sudden sound of the front door opening made my heart race.

I sat up, and Jaxon stirred beside me, his gaze meeting mine as we both listened to the voices echoing through the house. Glancing at the glowing clock on the nightstand, I saw it was one a.m.

Logan and the pack were home. Relief washed over me when I heard his voice; I was so excited to see my alphas again.

"Thank goodness they're back," I whispered, worry still lingering in my chest. Jaxon grinned lazily, his one eye closed.

I stood up from the nest, straightening my dress excitedly as I heard their footsteps rushing up the steps to see me.

"Slow down. She's probably sleeping," said Logan, but the bedroom door swung open to reveal Logan, Axel, Griffin, Tyler, and Talon, all bruised and disheveled, their clothes torn from battle.

"Oh my God," I squealed, rushing over to them.

"Hey, beautiful," said Logan, hugging me back. He smelled like sweat, blood, and war. It made my pussy throb as I smelled the powerful, wolfish scent of war reminding me that he risked his life to save me.

"You made it," I said, burying my face in his chest and feeling his arms to ensure he was really there. He was truly here in the flesh.

"We did," said Logan, nodding toward Tyler and the alphas. "Tyler finished him off."

I turned to Tyler next.

"Glad to see you're safe," said Tyler, nodding to me. I nodded back, not quite ready to forgive him.

"I'm fine," I assured him, noticing the blood seeping from his shoulder. "You should get that checked out."

"A shower will fix it," he replied calmly, though I could sense his pain. I blamed the marking by Jaxon for this confusing connection. With a nod, Tyler left for the shower, and I turned to Griffin, Talon, and Axel.

"I'm hungry as fuck," said Griffin after hugging me. "Should I cook a gigantic meal for us, babe?"

"I'm not hungry," I said, laughing. A little bit of hunger gnawed at me, but nausea overtook me as I thought about everything that had transpired. "Logan, what's going to happen to us now?"

"The compound is in chaos right now," said Logan. "I don't know what's going to happen. Unfortunately, Henry's omegas are going to feel the pain of his passing. They're going to suffer hard."

My heart ached for those poor omegas trapped with the burden of an unbreakable bond between alpha and omega. An omega couldn't move on after being marked, and I knew how horrible it would be for me if I were in their shoes.

Axel broke the silence, eyeing me with hunger. "I want to hug you so bad, but I'm sweaty as hell."

"It's okay," I giggled, recognizing his attempt to lighten the mood.

With a grin, he rushed off to another bathroom to shower. As I looked down at my stained dress, I realized I needed a bath as well. I wanted to erase everything about Henry, and anything he represented.

"I'll help you," said Logan, unzipping my hideous white fluffy dress. As it dropped to the ground, I felt relieved when the heavy weight was gone.

"So fucking beautiful," Jaxon said, watching me as I stood naked before these two alphas.

"Let's shower together," Logan suggested, and my heart began to race. "I need to touch your body and feel you against me."

"It sounds like a wonderful idea," I replied, and he took me by the hand to the main bathroom. Jaxon took my other hand.

"I'll join as well."

***

THE SHOWER WAS hot and steamy as I stood between the two gigantic alphas on the glass floor. Four shower jets from above sprayed over us while Logan caressed my breasts with a soapy loofah and Jaxon massaged my ass with his warm hands.

"This bathroom is the fanciest I've ever been in," I said, impressed by the marble walls and breathing hard from arousal.

"It is," murmured Logan, leaning in to kiss me on the mouth. The water drenched us both as we kissed while Jaxon squeezed my ass cheeks.

"Prettiest ass ever," Jaxon muttered, spreading my cheeks open while I was distracted by Logan's kiss. Logan's hands moved from my waist to my thighs.

"Spread your legs for me," Logan said huskily against my

wet lips. Turned on again, I obeyed, knowing I was giving full control to the two alphas.

Logan reached down to cup my pussy in his hand.

"Let's get your tiny hole clean enough to lick from," Jaxon said from behind as he knelt between my legs, keeping my ass cheeks spread wide with both hands.

I swallowed hard as Logan's finger delved between my folds.

"Warm," he muttered, wiggling his finger deeper into my pussy. "I need my cock inside you, babe. To make sure you're safe and sound with me."

"Okay," I breathed, while Jaxon rubbed my asshole with a soapy finger. "I like that idea."

Logan kissed me again when he removed his finger, and I reached for his cock. He was hard indeed, and my heart started to race because I was pretty big from pregnancy and had no idea how he planned to fuck me in the shower while standing.

Overcome by a wave of desire, my legs trembled beneath me.

"Damn," Jaxon muttered as he felt my muscles responding, clenching around the intrusion of his finger. His hand never left its spot on my ass, massaging circles into my sphincter with his thumb.

Simultaneously, Logan stroked himself slowly at first, then increased the pace when he heard me whimper from arousal and anticipation.

"You want us inside you?" Logan asked, his electrifying gaze making me nearly swoon.

"I do."

Lifting me with his powerful arms, he positioned me over his humongous throbbing cock.

"But you'll get tired- I'm very heavy," I cried out, my face flaming with embarrassment. But he silently speared my pussy with his length.

"Shh, baby, let me knot you," he said while Jaxon pushed another finger into my asshole, making me cry out. I suddenly felt the head of Jaxon's cock press against my asshole.

"Hold on," said Jaxon, penetrating my ass before Logan could begin thrusting into me. His cock stretched my asshole wider and wider with every inch of him.

"Oh fuck," I breathed.

"Little omegas shouldn't talk like that," said Jaxon, slapping my ass cheeks and shoving the rest of his cock into me.

"I'm sorry," I gasped, but Logan began lifting me up and down onto their cocks. The stretching of my pussy and ass was simultaneous as he thrust into me under the water.

"Fuck," grunted Logan as he pulled out and then back into my pussy while lifting me by the waist like I weighed nothing at all. I felt lighter than a feather as these two alphas handled me like a tiny doll between them.

I felt like I was flying as they lifted me up and down onto their cocks. My pussy and ass were being stretched like never before, and it felt so fucking good. The squelching sounds of my slick filled the space over the roaring water.

"Oh god," I said, arching my back so I could feel more of Logan's cock push deeper into my pussy. "It feels so good."

"I agree, baby," said Logan. "I made it through war just to feel your tight little pussy again."

He pistoned into me once more, roaring as jets of hot sperm flowed directly into my channel.

Jaxon thrust a couple more times, growling his release simultaneously as I cried out from his swelling cock in my ass. It didn't hurt, just felt mildly uncomfortable, as I felt both my pussy and ass stretching around their cocks.

"Fuck," said Jaxon, kissing the back of my wet shoulder while Logan kissed me on the lips hungrily.

"I don't want to be separated from you ever again," said Logan. "I love you so much."

"I love you too," I whispered back, kissing him while my heart pounded wildly from their touch and affection all over my body.

Jaxon squeezed my ass cheeks around his cock. "Sorry for crashing your shower session with our pack leader—but waking up next to you in the nest made me horny again."

"It's okay," I giggled while Logan squirted shampoo over my hair to help wash me.

"I'm not mad at you, Jax," said Logan gruffly as he massaged my scalp, and I melted under his touch. "Make yourself useful and shave our beautiful omega."

"Gladly," Jaxon replied behind me with a grin in his voice, and my face turned red.

AFTER AN HOUR in the shower and being knotted again, we were laughing as all three of us emerged from the bathroom wrapped in towels. Jaxon went into his room while Logan and I headed towards the main bedroom.

I suddenly bumped into Tyler, who was on his way downstairs. His eyes looked sorrowful when he saw the two alphas beside me.

My heart raced as I looked away from him and headed straight for the bedroom.

"Carmen?" Logan said, confusion evident as he followed me into the room.

"It's Tyler," I replied, trying to calm my breathing. "How the hell am I supposed to handle him here? I don't want him around."

"I'm sorry, babe," Logan said, gently touching my wet shoulders before kissing my forehead. "But he's part of the pack now and has pledged his allegiance. You have no choice but to trust him."

"Why would you even allow this to happen?" I asked, even though I already knew the answer.

"He loves you," Logan said simply. "And anyone who loves you will help protect you at all costs."

"But you didn't believe him before. What makes you so sure now?"

"I trust him now," Logan replied. "He wouldn't hurt you again. Not after everything. Everything he did was to protect you."

"Yeah, I don't believe it," I said, knowing that I would need to have a serious talk with him sooner rather than later. Now that Tyler was in the pack, it would be harder to avoid him and resist his scent, considering our past.

chapter 27

· · ·

Carmen

Logan left the room to eat dinner with the pack while I stayed upstairs, slathering lotion all over my body.

It sucked that all my things were in Florida, so I decided I'd just sleep naked tonight until we could do some shopping tomorrow.

The bedroom door opened again, and I gasped when I saw Tyler in the reflection of the mirror.

I scrambled to pick up my towel from the ground and quickly wrapped it around my body. It barely covered anything because of how big I was, but it was better than nothing.

"What do you want?" I asked, my voice sharper than I intended.

"I came to apologize. To clear the air."

I turned to face him. "How can we move on when you rejected me twice? It would be impossible to trust you again, Tyler."

"I understand. But I want you to know that I will do everything in my power to make it right," he said, his eyes sorrowful as he gazed at me.

"Tyler," I said, my voice barely audible as my heart pounded in my chest. "I don't feel comfortable around you."

His eyes widened, and he took a hesitant step back. "I'll do whatever it takes to make you feel comfortable. If that means leaving, I will."

My mind raced, torn between wanting him near and being unable to forget the pain his rejections had caused. *What would it be like to have him around, knowing we couldn't be happy together?* But the thought of him leaving again twisted my stomach with anxiety.

"No," I whispered, finally making up my mind. "You can stay. Just give me some space."

"Alright," Tyler said softly, relief evident in his voice. "I swear to you that I'll never break your heart again. We can sleep in separate rooms if that's what you need."

"Yeah, that's a good idea," I said.

He left the room, and I let out a long exhale after hearing the soft click of the door behind me. I was relieved that we didn't need to talk anymore tonight. Tyler sounded genuine, and while my heart felt moved by his words, I couldn't trust him at all yet.

Exhausted from the day's events, I decided to get some sleep while the alphas were eating downstairs and celebrating the defeat of Henry.

Slipping into the nest, I pulled the soft blanket to my chin, drifting off to thoughts of Tyler and how we would move forward, if at all.

IN THE MIDDLE of the night, I jolted awake, my body burning with a sudden surge of lust. Something huge filled my pussy, stretching me deliciously as I tried to make sense of the situation.

Groggily opening my eyes, I saw Griffin sleeping next to me, his chest rising and falling with even breaths. My legs were spread wide, one leg draped over his waist.

But his thick cock was buried deep inside me.

Did I freaking ride him in my sleep, or had he decided to insert himself inside me?

Panic mixed with arousal went through me as slick seeped from my pussy, coating Griffin's cock and making my hips twitch with needy desire.

I wanted friction and some movement of his cock inside me, despite how sleepy I was. The throbbing between my legs made it hard for me to fall back asleep.

Unable to resist the temptation any longer, I began to rock my hips, trying to ride Griffin's dick for some much-needed friction. The motion stirred him slightly, a low groan escaping his lips, but he didn't wake up.

My pulse raced with need as I lifted my belly to take him deep inside me.

"Fuck it," I whispered to myself. Reaching down, my fingers found my clit, swollen and sensitive. I circled it slowly at first as my pussy tightened around Griffin.

The room was filled with the sounds of my moans and whimpers, mixing with the alpha's snores. I could feel my orgasm building, making my legs tremble.

Suddenly, Griffin's eyes flashed open, and he flipped me onto my back. His hands gripped my hips as he drove into me, pushing me further and further toward the edge.

"Did you need some help, sweet thing?" he asked as he thrust into me.

"Griff," I cried out, my voice cracking as I rubbed my clit furiously. "I woke up, and you were inside me."

"I needed you to warm my cock," he whispered into my ear, biting my earlobe. I tensed before finally shattering with my orgasm.

He came too, grunting as he thrust into me a couple more times. Wave after wave of pleasure washed over me, leaving me breathless and spent. As the last tremors of my orgasm faded, I collapsed against the pillow, my slick-covered fingers still tangled in my sex.

"That was..."

"Fucking hot," he growled, kissing me on the lips. "I love you, sweetheart."

"I love you too," I whispered in the dark.

chapter 28

. . .

Tyler

The next morning, I stood at the top of the staircase, watching our omega, Carmen, laughing in the kitchen. Her voice was melodic and beautiful to my ears, and I wished I could be around her.

She was surrounded by some of the alphas who were helping her cook breakfast.

Even though I didn't want to intrude on her happiness, I couldn't tear my eyes away from the way her body moved. The swell of her pregnant belly made her dress ride up higher than it should have, revealing her tantalizing curves.

As she bent down to retrieve a spoon that had fallen to the floor, the sight of her black thong peeking out from beneath the hem of her dress sent a bolt of lust through me.

My cock strained against my pants, and I licked my lips, desperate to taste her. But I knew I couldn't just take her, not after all the hurt I'd caused.

A heavy sadness settled over me as I quietly mourned the distance between us.

The doorbell rang, and now I was on alert.

"Who is it?" said Logan, opening the door.

A woman stood there wearing a gray sweater dress. I recognized her as Carmen's mother. She didn't look happy as she stormed inside, rage emanating from her.

She beelined toward Carmen in the kitchen, and I straightened up, ready to jump down the stairs to protect her.

"What did you do?! Why is Henry dead?" she screamed at Carmen.

Rage roared through me like a wildfire, and before I knew it, my feet were pounding down the stairs.

A pained silence replaced Carmen's laughter, tears in her eyes while her mother glowered at her. I couldn't let Carmen be subjected to this cruelty.

"Leave her alone," I growled, stepping protectively in front of Carmen. "None of this has anything to do with her. We destroyed the scumbag."

"She was supposed to be for Henry," shouted Carmen's mother, staring daggers at Carmen. "If you people had just let her be with Henry, my family would have been royalty!"

"What the fuck?" I muttered, realizing this woman was deranged.

We stood there, tense with unspoken words, our gazes locked in fierce confrontation. Then, Carmen placed a soft hand on my arm.

Her touch went straight to my soul, and I felt my anger dissipate as quickly as it had come.

"Let me talk to my mom, Tyler," she whispered, her voice soft against the harsh beating of my heart. "Please."

I took a deep breath and reluctantly backed off, feeling the urge to protect Carmen more than ever. I wanted to mark her, claim her, knot her, and keep her all to myself. But I knew she needed to handle this situation on her own terms.

"I won't be far," I growled, standing right there in the kitchen.

Carmen

MY HEART POUNDED as I looked into my mother's tear-filled eyes. She stared at my pregnant belly, her expression a mix of shock and disgust. I knew she was obsessed with Henry, but I couldn't let her continue to believe that he was anything but a monster.

"Mom," I said softly. "Henry was a horrible alpha. He's the reason I couldn't live here at the compound."

I could see Tyler talking with Logan on the other side of the kitchen, but I felt Tyler's energy entirely on me. He was observing in case things got out of hand.

"You never gave Henry a chance!"

"He's dead now, Mom."

Her lips formed a firm line, and it seemed like she struggled to accept the truth.

"This is crazy," she said, looking around at the six alphas who were either hanging out in the kitchen or living room. They were pretending not to listen in on the conversation, and I wanted to smile as my heart warmed from their overprotectiveness.

"Have breakfast with me," I said, placing a hand over my belly. "And you can meet my pack."

"Fine," she said, glancing at my belly as we made our way to the dining table. I could see the gears in her mind, thinking about the future grandchild I carried.

Axel placed a cup of tea before her while I carried my cup in my hand. We talked for hours as the alphas busied themselves around the massive house. A couple of my alphas were outside, and some were at the pool. But I could sense Tyler still standing in the living room, keeping an eye on us, which made my heart beat a little faster.

I sat on the couch, lost in thought after my mom left. It seemed like she was okay following our discussion. At first, it was hard for her to accept that Henry was really gone, but once I told her that he wanted to take me by force, that made her upset.

After she left the house, Tyler also departed after deciding in his mind that I was safe.

"Hey," Griffin said softly as he entered the living room, concern etched on his face. He sat down next to me and wrapped his arm around my waist, pulling me closer. "What's the matter?"

Leaning against his chest, I sighed. "I never thought I'd end up with six alphas."

He chuckled, his breath ruffling my hair. "Isn't that a good thing for you? You'll be the most protected omega around."

"I have to make sure I take care of every alpha's emotions," I said, knowing that as an omega, my job was to keep my alphas satiated and happy.

I felt physically and emotionally empty, unsure how to navigate things with Tyler.

"Hmm, the only thing left for you to do is to forgive the bloke," Griffin said in a low voice as I played with his beard while he rubbed my belly.

He knew that I was talking about Tyler.

I clenched my thighs together, feeling aroused all of a sudden, as if a weight had been lifted. Just then, Jaxon strolled into the room.

"I can smell you, honey," Jaxon said, his eyes filled with hunger and desire. Without a word, he knelt between my legs and lifted my dress. Griffin's hand rubbed my bare thigh, spreading me wide for Jaxon.

"There she is," grunted Griffin as he watched Jaxon rub my pussy over my thong.

"Our honey is wet," said Jaxon, pushing his head between my thighs. The sensation of Jaxon's tongue exploring my folds made me widen my legs even more. It felt like electricity, igniting every nerve ending and building intense pressure deep within me.

Griffin played with my breasts, pinching my nipple while his other hand held me tightly. He captured my moans in a passionate kiss, muffling the sounds of ecstasy as Jaxon devoured me.

"Mhm," I moaned against Griffin's lips.

"God, you taste so good," Jaxon growled, his voice low and rough. "I can't get enough of you."

Suddenly, he ripped my thong in half with his teeth, and I gasped at the suddenness of it all, my heart racing like a drum.

He began licking my bare pussy.

"Eat her out. Vigorously," said Griffin, watching as he touched himself, his massive cock already out. Jaxon's tongue swirled around my clit until I moaned loudly, allowing my thighs to fall open as I leaned back on the couch.

"Oh fuck," I gasped, screaming as my orgasm tore through me. My thighs shook, and my belly clenched, but he continued licking every drop of slick that expelled from me. "Oh my god, stop."

I was left trembling and weak as Jaxon looked up at me, his face smeared with my arousal, a devilish grin on his lips.

"Tasty omega."

"Oh god," I breathed, my body still quivering from the intensity of the orgasm. Jaxon smirked, clearly pleased with himself.

Just as I was about to get off the couch to take a quick shower, Griffin pulled me onto his lap.

"I thought we were done," I whispered hoarsely.

"I want to knot you, babe. Touch my dick," he said, and I smiled, breathing hard as I wrapped my fingers around his firmness.

Suddenly, I felt a pair of hands squeezing my cheeks open. I was used to these alphas catching me by surprise. Turning my head, I saw a feral Axel staring at my ass, his cock standing erect.

As I turned back around, Griffin captured my lips with his, kissing me as he slid his giant cock into my already primed and wet pussy. Griffin growled as my pussy clenched around him, awakening his primal need as he filled me.

"Such a pretty little ass," said Axel, beginning to rub my anus in circles. My breath hitched when I felt slick moistening my entrance, lubricating me before Axel would thrust into me from behind. He was kneeling on the ground, and I suddenly felt his tongue press against my asshole.

"Oh god," I said as Griffin's cock pulsed inside me while Axel played with my sphincter. His tongue was wide as he licked up and down my crack.

"Fuck. So fucking good," said Axel, pressing his tongue into my hole as I gripped Griffin's upper arms with a gasp. "Clenching so tight. Relax for me, baby."

"Is he making you feel good, hun?" asked Griffin, who was absorbed in kissing and smelling my neck.

I took a few deep breaths to relax my ass for Axel so they could both thrust into me at the same time. His tongue pressed deeper into my ass as my nails dug into Griffin's arms.

Suddenly, I felt something pressing against the side of my cheek, and I looked around to see another cock wanting attention.

"Oh, moons," I said, seeing Talon standing there with fire in his eyes. His hair was wet from the pool, but he was more than ready to be pleasured.

"I need some too, omega," he said, and I willingly opened

my mouth to take him in. He was so big that my jaw had no room to close as he pushed in a few inches.

Soon, the tongue in my ass was replaced with Axel's cock, and the three alphas began slowly, pulling in and out. Griffin growled as he lifted me up and then down onto his dick.

Axel used my movement for his enjoyment with my very stretched asshole.

I looked up into Talon's eyes as I swirled the tip of his cock with my tongue, enjoying every moment of his growls of pleasure.

"Just like that, baby," he said, gripping my hair. When he did that, I suddenly saw Tyler standing at the top of the staircase, watching me.

Oh, fuck me.

My pulse raced, and I lost all concentration, starting to choke on Talon's dick. Talon immediately pulled his cock out of my mouth.

"You okay, baby?" he asked, touching my cheek with concern. "Sorry if I was too much."

"No, it's fine," I said, my cheeks flaming as I turned my attention back to Talon. From the corner of my eye, I saw Tyler smirking, but I chose to ignore him as Talon slid back into my mouth.

I hollowed out my cheeks as I sucked him.

"Fuck," growled Griffin, lifting me up powerfully and slamming me back down onto his cock, stretching my pussy. I moaned while sucking on Talon's cock.

Axel continued to pound into my ass, his balls making slapping sounds against my cheeks. "So fucking tight. Good omega."

"She is," crooned Talon from above as he stroked my cheeks while my mouth dribbled with his cum. "A very good girl."

I swallowed quickly as he pulled out, nearly choking again

when Griffin slammed me one more time onto his dick. Axel pistoned into my ass, and they both roared at the same time as hot streams of liquid filled my pussy and ass. Their cocks began to swell, stretching me widely until I moaned with exhaustion, falling against Axel's chest.

"Fuck," Tyler growled from above as he also came using his hand while watching us.

chapter 29

. . .

Carmen

A few days later, the sun streamed through the window, casting a golden glow on my nest of cushions in the corner of the room. I was curled up with a steamy romance novel, losing myself in the story while my alphas were busy with work and running errands.

I had gotten as comfortable as I could without all my stuff back in Florida. It had been a couple of days since we returned to the Alpha Compound, and my alphas had been spoiling me rotten, buying me clothes and anything else I needed.

With six powerful alphas at my beck and call, I couldn't help but feel like a queen. Suddenly, I heard the sound of rolling wheels and footsteps outside my bedroom door.

"Yes?"

"It's Tyler."

My heart started to pound faster. I had taken a strict stance with him, not giving him an inch of softness.

"Okay," I replied, glancing up to see Tyler entering, carrying my suitcases from Florida.

He paused, looking at me all cozy in my nest as he set the suitcases down. "I brought your things."

"Oh, that's why you were gone yesterday," I said.

"Yeah."

"Well, thank you," I said, momentarily touched by the fact that he cared enough to do this.

"You're welcome," he said, turning to leave. Something about his sad expression made my heart break.

"Wait, don't go," I blurted out, setting my book aside. My pulse raced as he turned back to face me, his green eyes searching mine for answers.

"What is it, Carmen?" he asked, concern etched across his face. There were bags under his eyes, and they were red—looking like he hadn't slept in days.

"Tyler," I whispered as tears pricked my eyes. "Have you slept at all?"

"It's nothing for you to worry about," he said quickly, looking off to the side in a stoic alpha manner.

"Come," I said, patting the cushion beside me. Even though I was hurt by how he had treated me in the past, I didn't like seeing him so tense.

"Are you sure?" he asked, hesitating to come near me.

"I'm sure, Ty," I said, biting my lip as he approached my nest slowly. His cedar scent enveloped me the moment he joined me, and the heat radiating from his body made my skin tingle. I could feel the tension between us, crackling in the air.

"What's on your mind?" he urged, his voice soft.

"Why haven't you been sleeping?" I asked, wanting to take his hand but feeling scared. I was terrified of what that would imply after our recent feud.

He looked at me with a hooded expression that made my heart race faster. "You're on my mind. Constantly."

My heart trembled as Tyler's eyes softened at the sight of my tears. He reached up, gently catching a tear with the pad of his thumb before it could trail down my cheek.

"Really?"

"Carmen," he murmured, his voice thick with emotion, "I love you. I've never stopped loving you since the day we met."

"Then why?" I asked, hating that my voice trembled so weakly. "Why did you let go of our love so easily?"

He sighed, twirling my hair between his fingers. "To protect you. To get the job as Henry's security guard, I didn't want the omega I love around him. Knowing how he is, that would have been dangerous."

I didn't know how to feel at his admission. If what he said was true, then that meant he had always loved me, and we were always meant to be.

"So you did care," I said in a low voice, remembering the letters that I had seen—the letters he never sent me.

"You are my priority," he said, his voice full of sorrow and sincerity.

As our eyes locked, I could feel the intensity of his gaze melting away the walls I'd built around my heart. Slowly, I inched closer to him, maintaining eye contact even though my stomach was somersaulting.

"May I?" Tyler asked, his gaze lowering to my mouth. I nodded, and he covered my lips with his in a hungry kiss. The large alpha wrapped his arm around me, pulling me closer as we kissed desperately. I placed a hand over his chest, feeling his heart race like mine.

"Stay with me," I begged, my fingers gripping his shirt, afraid he would slip away if I let go.

"Of course," he whispered against my lips, pulling me into his embrace. "I'll stay as long as you need me."

I STARED into Tyler's eyes, the intensity in them burning away any remaining doubts I had about his feelings for me. My heart swelled with love as I kept my hand on his chest, feeling the steady rhythm of his heartbeat beneath my palm.

"You really did protect me," I whispered, my voice thick with emotion.

"My life's mission," he promised, pulling me closer until our bodies were pressed together, our breaths mingling.

The air between us grew heavy with desire, which we had suppressed for days.

As if drawn by an irresistible force, his lips found mine again in a rough, passionate kiss. Tyler's low growl reverberated through me, sending shivers down my spine. I moaned into his mouth, feeling the hardness of his lips against my own, the sensation electrifying.

"God, Carmen," he muttered between kisses, his hands roaming over my body, tracing the curves of my hips, the swell of my breasts, and my pregnant belly.

The heat from his touch seared through my skin, leaving me panting for more.

"Tyler... I want you," I gasped. He kissed me again, and our tongues danced around each other, the taste of him igniting a hunger within me that only he could satisfy. His strong arms enveloped me, as if trying to merge our bodies into one.

"Tell me what you want," he breathed into my ear, nipping at my lobe with a teasing bite. His words sent tremors through my core, and I knew there was no turning back.

"I want you, Tyler. All of you," I whispered, my heart pounding a thousand miles a minute.

His eyes darkened, and the predatory gleam within them sent a thrill of anticipation coursing through me.

"Then you'll have me," he promised, his voice rough with need.

I straddled his waist and tried to free his erection from his sweatpants.

His hands caressed my waist, making me shiver.

"Carmen, I don't just want to fuck you senseless," he murmured, his voice low and full of emotion. "I want to make love to you, to worship every inch of your body, and show you how much you mean to me."

Tyler gently picked me up and laid me down on my back in the nest.

My breathing quickened as he started pulling down my leggings while pressing soft kisses against my thighs and belly, leaving goosebumps in their wake.

"Your underwear is soaked," he commented with a hint of mischief in his voice. "What kind of book were you reading?"

I blushed, burying my face in my hands for a moment before admitting, "It's just a romance book."

Tyler traced a finger along the edge of my panties, sending shivers up my spine.

"And what were the characters doing in this book that got you so worked up?" he asked, his touch becoming bolder as he rubbed my pussy through my underwear.

"Uhm, well... they were, uh, kissing and touching each other all over," I stammered, my heart racing as his skilled fingers continued to tease me, causing my pussy to clench and release more slick. "The alpha was whispering sweet nothings into his omega's ear, telling her how beautiful she was and how much he wanted her."

"Like this?" Tyler whispered, his lips brushing against my ear as he spoke. "You're so incredibly beautiful, Carmen, and I want you more than anything in this world. What else was the alpha doing to her?"

My breath hitched as my pussy clenched with him playing with it like he owned it. I could hardly focus.

"He put his fingers inside of her," I whispered, the heat from his mouth tracing along my jaw.

"Would you like me to do the same for you?" Tyler asked,

his voice low and seductive. My cheeks flushed even more as he slowly pulled my underwear down over my thick thighs and off my legs, his eyes never leaving mine.

"Yes," I said as he kissed my inner thighs, his warm lips pressing against my skin.

"Look at how wet you are," he growled, holding up my soaked panties. "Were you just thinking about naughty things this whole time you were alone in your nest?"

My face couldn't get any redder than it was in that moment.

"I was," I admitted, embarrassed. Being with Tyler felt like being with a whole new alpha, making me shy.

I felt like a virgin all over again.

Without warning, he pressed my panties against his nose, inhaling deeply. The sight of him doing that made me clench my thighs as a bolt of arousal shot through me.

"Tyler, stop it!" I said, feeling embarrassed- but he only growled in response, breathing in my lime aroma once more as he pressed my purple panties harder against his nose.

"Your scent is... I can't get enough," he admitted huskily, his desire for me evident in his voice. "I can't help myself."

He reluctantly dropped my underwear onto the carpet and turned his attention back to me. His fiery gaze lowered to my pussy as he rubbed a hand over my little hairs. He started to rub my thighs, his strong hands gently coaxing my trembling legs apart.

"Sorry, I'm just a little nervous," I said in a shaky voice. "We haven't done it... in months."

"I will fix that mistake," he growled. "You'll get used to me again, and you'll have to get re-acquainted with my cock."

He admired my pussy after helping me spread my shaking thighs- then began to gently stroke my labia, taking his time to explore every inch of my lips.

"So fucking beautiful," he murmured under his breath as

he spread my pussy lips open. I was so aroused that I couldn't help the slick seeping out of me, as if I were in heat again. He leaned down, licking my pussy in long strokes, making me moan in my nest.

Tyler pushed a finger into my channel, stretching me with the thickness of his finger. His black ring pressed against my clit as he thrust his middle finger into me.

Suddenly, his mouth moved to my inner thigh, and I felt his sharp teeth ready to mark me. My heart pounded harder in anticipation as he quickly bit into my skin.

"Oh my god," I cried out as I felt his venom mix into my blood, shooting through me to form our permanent bond.

"My omega," he growled, licking the painful spot. He lifted his head to wipe away a tear I hadn't noticed running down my face. "The pain will be worth it, my love."

Soon enough, just like my other marking, the pain dwindled, but my arousal increased. I spread my thighs wider for him as I circled my clitoris with a finger.

"Please, Tyler," I begged breathlessly, my chest heaving with each panting breath. "I need you inside me."

As Tyler positioned himself between my trembling thighs, I could feel the tip of his cock pressing against my slick entrance.

"Are you ready for me, Carmen?" he asked with restrained desire.

"Yes," I whispered, my eyes locking with his as my breathing quickened.

With a slow, deliberate motion, Tyler pushed his length inside me, filling me completely. The delicious stretch of his cock within me made my breath catch in my throat, and I couldn't help but release a soft moan. He paused for a moment, allowing me to adjust to his size before tenderly thrusting deeper.

"So fucking amazing," he groaned, his breath hot against my skin as he moved within me.

Each thrust was slow and deep, making my entire body tremble with pleasure.

I gripped his ass cheeks to pull him in deeper because I wanted more of him. He chuckled darkly as he thrust all the way into me, and I gasped.

"Tyler, you're huge."

"Isn't that what you like? Did you miss me, darling?"

"Yes," I moaned as his hips pistoned into me with increasing urgency. My pussy stretched around his cock, hugging him tighter with each thrust. "Oh my god, don't stop."

He grunted, his face tense as he thrust faster and faster.

Pushing in deeper, inch by inch.

"Fuck," he growled as spurts of his hot semen filled me. "Fuck, Carmen."

"Oh, Ty," I moaned as he kissed me hard while his cock pumped deep inside me. Soon the base of his cock began to swell, knotting us together as he grunted with pleasure. "Feels so good."

Finally, Tyler let out a deep growl as his knot fully formed, locking us together in the most intimate way possible. My body shook from the intensity of our connection, and I felt tears prickling at the corners of my eyes.

"Are you okay?" Tyler asked gently, brushing my damp hair away from my face as he looked down at me with concern.

"Better than okay," I whispered softly, smiling through my tears. "I've never felt so connected to anyone in my entire life."

"Neither have I," he admitted, his eyes softening as he lay beside me with his cock still inside me. And it would be like that for the next thirty minutes. "I love you, Carmen."

"I love you too," I said, and saying the words felt easy. It wasn't forced, and I felt the connection radiating deep into my bones.

chapter 30

. . .

Carmen

couple of weeks later, we flew out to Florida, leaving the Alpha Compound behind as we fled from toxic family dynamics in search of a fresh start. Tyler's mother was furious when she found out about my pregnancy, which made our decision to leave even more necessary.

I sat in the passenger's seat, glancing at Logan as he drove. We weren't headed to our usual rental home, which I assumed was our destination.

"Where are we going?" I asked, curiously watching the palm trees zoom by.

"It's a surprise, baby," said Logan, winking at me. Axel and Jaxon were sitting in the backseat, and I could feel the alphas' excitement in the air.

"Ugh, you know I hate surprises," I complained, folding my arms over my growing pregnant belly. I felt like I might burst in this dress if I didn't get to rip it off soon.

Logan chuckled, his deep laugh sending warmth through me. "I know. Just relax and enjoy the ride, Carmen. Maybe turn on some music to calm your nerves?"

I sighed but reached for the radio, flipping through

stations until I found one playing upbeat tunes. As the music filled the car, I felt Jaxon's presence behind me and glanced back.

His hazel eyes held an intense, almost predatory gaze as they locked onto mine.

He leaned forward, reaching around my seat and under my dress. I gasped when I felt his fingers bury into the thin panties I was wearing.

"Jax, someone might see us," I gasped, looking around at all the windows. We were driving down a highway, and cars were zooming past us, making me feel self-conscious with a large alpha hand outlined beneath my dress.

"I'll help you relax, baby," he growled into my ear from behind as he rubbed my folds in circles. His touch sent a jolt of arousal through my body, causing slick to pool between my thighs. "Fuck if anyone sees. Let them watch how it's done."

I clutched the door handle tightly, my breaths becoming shallow and ragged.

Then he immediately lifted my dress with his other hand, and I squealed in shock. "Jaxon!"

I tried to pull my dress down to cover myself because I was now completely exposed with his hand deep inside my underwear. I couldn't tug my dress down because of his tight hold.

"Logan," I whined in panic.

"Dude," said Logan. "Do you want the world to see her? That's only for us."

Jaxon groaned as he reluctantly released my dress, and I quickly covered myself again, breathing hard from the adrenaline.

"Shh, baby. Open for me."

With gentle precision, he circled his fingers around my sensitive clit, eliciting moans from deep within me. As he slid two fingers inside my tight core, I felt my pussy stretching as he pumped me. I bit down on my lip, trying to contain the ecstasy building within me. My body tensed and writhed under his touch, each stroke of his thick fingers bringing me closer to the edge.

"Jaxon," I whimpered, unable to hold back any longer. I tried to maintain a poker face but failed, quickly covering my face as the dam burst within me.

Jaxon's fingers continued to pump inside me until every last tremor had faded away. I slumped against the seat, panting heavily, my vision blurry from the intensity of my release.

"Feeling better now?" Logan asked, rubbing my thighs as Jaxon slowly withdrew his fingers from my pussy. I looked back at Jaxon to give him a piece of my mind about the dress situation, but my face heated when I saw him licking his fingers clean.

"Mhm, delicious."

"Oh my god," I muttered, turning back to face the front, breathing hard while my pussy clenched in response to the aftershocks.

TEN MINUTES LATER, we finally reached our destination, and I stared at the massive house in awe as Logan pulled into the driveway.

"Oh wow, is this our new rental?" I asked out loud. The alphas didn't answer me. Axel came around to open my door and helped me out of the van. I hugged him tight with excitement for our vacation, and he chuckled, surprised.

Tyler approached me, holding a key in his hand.

"Here," he said softly, placing the key into my palm. Confusion clouded my mind as I looked down at the key.

"Why are you giving me the key?" I asked.

Tyler smiled warmly, his blue eyes filled with affection. "I bought you a house, Carmen. Welcome home."

Tears welled up in my eyes as I clutched the key, overwhelmed by Tyler's gesture.

"You didn't have to do this," I whispered, trying to blink back the tears.

"Yes, I did," he insisted, his voice thick with emotion. "You deserve this—even though you deserve so much more."

I shook my head, still unable to grasp the enormity of his gift.

An entire house he bought for me.

"Tyler," I started, but then I saw his eyes cloud with a darkness I couldn't explain.

"Every day, I hate myself for what I did to you," he choked out, the pain in his voice cutting through me like a knife. There were actual tears in his eyes, even though I begged him not to torture himself over our past. "Will you forgive me, Carmen?"

"Tyler," I said softly, my heart aching as tears filled my own eyes. I cupped his face in my hands, compelling him to meet my gaze. "I forgave you a long time ago."

His eyes shimmered with unshed tears, and without another word, we kissed deeply, our connection stronger than ever before. The baby seemed to sense it, kicking gently inside me. I guided Tyler's hand to my belly, and we both smiled through our tears as we felt the life within me while we stood there silently for a few minutes.

"Thank you for forgiving me," said Tyler, and I nodded.

"The moment we step into the house, we won't ever bring it up again," I said vehemently. "We're going to start fresh."

He smiled, clearly liking my idea, giving my hand a squeeze. "Let's go inside then, my love."

We all walked into our new house, and I was immediately struck by its beauty.

The open floor plan, gleaming hardwood floors, and state-of-the-art appliances made the space feel like a dream come true.

Despite the lack of furniture, I could already envision the warm colors I would choose to transform it into a home for us and the new baby on the way.

"Can you believe this place?" I exclaimed, my eyes darting around the spacious living area. "It's so beautiful, and there's enough space for all of us. There would be enough space for my sisters to visit, too."

The alphas couldn't help but smile at my enthusiasm.

Talon took advantage of my momentary distraction to lean in and steal a quick kiss. His scent enveloped me—a unique blend of earth and spice that was so undeniably him.

"Looks like we'll be staying here for a while," Talon mused. "I love seeing you so happy."

"I agree," chimed in Jaxon as he checked out the veranda.

"I would have to move my fitness gym here," said Axel.

"And my art studio," added Logan, taking my hand.

As we stood there discussing our new lives together, Logan suddenly dropped down onto one knee. My heart raced, and my breath caught in my throat. Before I could fully process the situation, the other alphas followed suit, surrounding me as they all knelt around me.

Tears welled in my eyes before he even started talking.

"Sweet Carmen," he began, his dark eyes locked on mine. "From the moment we met, you've captivated me. We started as best friends, but now we stand here, bonded by love and a baby."

My heart pounded in my chest as tears filled my eyes. Logan's voice was smooth and confident, and each word was carefully chosen to make me feel cherished.

"Oh my god," I muttered to myself, feeling overwhelmed by the love emanating from each of the alphas.

"I want nothing more than to spend the rest of my life

protecting you and sharing in our love for one another," he continued, opening a small ring box to reveal a stunning diamond ring that glittered in the sunlight. My breath caught in my throat. The ring featured six blue gems surrounding a giant diamond in the middle.

"Each of the smaller stones represents one of us, and the central rock is you, Carmen," explained Axel.

"Will you marry us, Carmen, and become an eternal omega of our pack? Will you say yes to every alpha here?" he asked gruffly, his voice filled with emotion.

Tears flowed freely down my cheeks as I choked out a single word, "Yes." I wanted to scream with joy, but I held out my trembling left hand as Logan slid the heavy ring onto my finger.

The alphas all rose, happiness lighting up their faces at my acceptance of their proposal. One by one, I kissed each of them tenderly on the lips, feeling the heat of desire build between us.

"I'm your fiancé now," said Jaxon as he kissed me with fervor, making my heart race. "Shall we have our first knotting in our brand new home?"

"But is there a bed?" I asked, laughing—my breath catching a little short because of my pregnancy.

"It sure does," said Axel, his voice deep.

"Eek," I squealed when both he and Jaxon carried me into the bedroom, where a large bed covered in intricate purple sheets awaited.

They gently laid me down on my back.

"You're going to look so pretty spread for the pack," said Jaxon. "Who's going to knot her first?"

"Me," said Logan simply, and my body quivered with anticipation as Jaxon and Axel each held one of my legs up. They spread me wide, allowing Logan to position himself between my thighs. The intensity in his eyes made my heart race wildly, and I could feel slick rushing down my pussy.

"Are you ready for him?" asked Axel, and I nodded.

As Logan entered me slowly, the sensation of being stretched just for him caused a wave of pleasure in my belly. I moaned loudly, unable to hold back my desire.

Tyler and Griffin joined us on the bed, playing with my breasts.

"Stretched and beautiful," Tyler whispered into my ear as he sucked on my left breast. "You're taking our pack leader in very well."

Meanwhile, Axel and Tyler took turns sucking on my breasts, their mouths warm and insistent. They both played with my nipples in different ways – Tyler gently teasing them with his teeth while Axel swirled his tongue around them, sending bolts of pleasure straight to my core.

Griffin's lips found my thighs, leaving a trail of hot, open-mouthed kisses that contrasted deliciously with the cool air. As Logan thrust into me, Griffin's hands gripped my hips, helping to guide my body in sync with Logan's powerful movements.

"Your pussy feels fucking amazing," Logan growled, his voice filled with raw desire for me. "I can't get enough of you."

As I moaned in pleasure, Logan reached down to play with my clit, his fingers expertly manipulating the sensitive nub, amplifying the sensations coursing through my body.

"Oh, Logan, don't stop," I gasped, my body shaking from the intense pleasure.

Suddenly, Tyler decided it was time to explore another part of my body. He released my nipple from his mouth and shifted his attention to my ass.

As he gently spread my cheeks apart, I felt exposed but also incredibly aroused. Logan slowed his thrusts and then carefully pulled out, allowing them to position me onto my side.

Logan captured my mouth in a passionate kiss, drinking in my moans while Tyler's fingers began pressing around my asshole, making me slick.

"She's wet," said Tyler, rubbing my anus in circles.

"Is her ass ready?" Logan asked impatiently, his voice low and urgent.

"Give me a minute," Tyler responded, but as I looked up at Logan, I saw the barely restrained lust in his dark eyes- he wasn't going to wait for long, and he would keep thrusting.

As Tyler continued to tease and stretch my hole with his fingers, I suddenly felt more slick pouring out of my ass, making it even easier for him to explore my asshole. The combination of pleasure and anticipation left me breathless, knowing that soon, I would be giving myself entirely to the alphas who had claimed my heart and body.

chapter 31

. . .

Tyler

"Tyler, she's so fucking ready for you," said Logan, his voice dripping with lust. "Tell him you're ready, Carmen, because I'm about to fucking explode."

"I'm... I'm ready," she gasped, feeling the intensity of the alphas ready to claim her.

I couldn't wait any longer as I gripped her ass cheeks firmly in my large hands. My cock was hard as fuck as I began massaging her ass cheeks apart. I squeezed the middle of her cheeks, spreading her slick around, thoroughly coating her.

Her scent was intoxicating, and I couldn't resist sinking my teeth into her shoulder, marking her as mine again. The taste of her blood on my tongue made me even more ravenous. Carmen moaned in pain, but it only seemed to heighten her arousal.

"Tell me what you want," I rasped, ready to fuck her tight little hole and make it mine.

"I want you to knot me," she said shyly. "In my ass."

"You look so beautiful like this," I murmured, touching myself as I took in the sight of her quivering asshole.

Griffin captured her lips in a passionate kiss, and I took that moment to penetrate her with my cock.

The tightness of Carmen's hole pulled me in, and I was lost in the exquisite feeling of being inside her ass. I groaned as I gripped her cheeks tighter, spreading her wider. My cock throbbed within her, the heat and pressure gripping me like a vice.

"Fuck," roared Logan as he continued to thrust into her pussy.

"So fucking tight," I growled, pushing myself deeper into her ass until I reached my limit. Carmen gasped against Griffin's mouth, her body shuddering with pleasure.

As I continued to thrust into her, I couldn't help but take in the scene around us—Griffin kissing Carmen passionately and the sound of her moans filling the room. Logan filling her little pussy. It was everything I'd been craving and more.

I pulled my cock back, then plunged deep into Carmen's ass again. I noticed Axel and Talon touching themselves as they watched us, their desire evident in their movements.

"Talon," I ordered. "Fill our omega's mouth."

Talon inched toward Carmen's face, the intensity of his gaze focused on her as he pushed his cock into her waiting mouth. With her mouth full, I thrust faster into her, ensuring her anal walls were still coated in slick to ease my passage.

"Logan!" she moaned around Talon's cock, her voice muffled by his length. I could feel the tension building within me, and I knew I wouldn't last much longer.

"You're going to take my cock in your little behind," I growled, my climax overtaking me, roaring as I held her ass cheeks open, feeling the heat and pressure intensify as my cock exploded inside her.

My breathing was heavy and ragged, sweat covering my body from the exertion.

I collapsed behind her, pressing gentle kisses to her shoul-

...ile she gulped down Talon's semen, white dribbles ...ping down her chin as she struggled to keep up.

"Such a good omega," I whispered sweetly into her ear, praising her as I pushed myself deeper into her, knotting inside her clenching ass. She moaned, arching her hips tighter against my knot.

Griffin

I PLAYED with Carmen's hair as I watched Talon cup the side of Carmen's face.

"Such a good omega," groaned Talon as he pulled himself out of Carmen's mouth. Her wide eyes at his praise made my cock harder.

"Guys," I said, watching as Logan slid out of Carmen. "I'll knot her pussy next."

Logan lifted Carmen's leg, granting me better access while she lay on her side. I couldn't help but admire her pink, glistening pussy, dripping with cum.

I licked my lips as Logan's seed slid down to her ass cheeks, where Tyler was still tightly knotted in.

"So fucking beautiful," I murmured with a hungry smile. "So beautiful covered in your pack's cum."

"It's a little embarrassing," she said, blushing as I watched her pussy dripping onto the sheets.

Carmen's breaths were ragged, her chest heaving as she tried to catch her breath. I reached out with the corner of a pillowcase and gently wiped the white dribble from her chin, concern lacing my voice.

"Are you okay?"

Her eyes met mine, glazed over with hazy lust. "More than okay. Please knot me, Griffin."

I couldn't help but smile at her enthusiasm. She was so fucking sexy.

"You make the perfect omega," I praised, watching as her cheeks flushed a pretty shade of pink. "Do you like being called a good girl? I noticed that when Talon called you that."

"Kind of. It turns me on," she said, biting her lip.

"Well, you are a good girl. Especially with your legs spread so wide for us. A very good girl," I crooned as I tried pushing the semen back into her swollen pussy.

Even though she was already pregnant, I didn't want any alpha's seed to go to waste. Gently pushing against her entrance, I tried to force the spilling liquid back inside her while she was sandwiched between Tyler and me on the bed.

"Oh," she breathed.

"Ready for me to knot you?" I asked, my cock throbbing with need. I was ready to plunge myself into her and thrust into her pussy for as long as fucking possible.

"Yes," she said, her breasts heaving eagerly with desire.

Positioning myself at her entrance, I began massaging her breast with one hand, delighting in the way her nipple hardened beneath my touch. As I pushed my dick inside her slick pussy, I was overwhelmed by the sensation of her warm, tight walls hugging my cock instantly.

"Fuck, that feels so good," Carmen moaned, licking her lips in pleasure. "Fuck me, Griffin."

"Amazing," I agreed, my voice strained with desire. "So fucking amazing."

Pushing my cock further into her pussy, I began to thrust deep inside her, starting slow and then picking up the pace. I pulled back and drove in at a rapid rhythm, her moans urging me on.

"Oh, Griff!" she screamed, still knotted by the ass as I drove my hips forward. The sound of her calling my name drove me wild, and I could feel the pressure of my climax building inside me.

Her pussy walls squeezed around me, gripping me tighter than anything I'd ever felt before. It was like I was riding an intoxicating high, the pleasure overwhelming my senses and pushing me closer to the edge.

Finally, I couldn't take it any longer.

With a roar, I exploded inside her just as she screamed in ecstasy. The intensity of our shared climax left me breathless, my heart pounding in my chest as I tried to regain my composure.

My heart thumped hard in my chest as I felt the base of my cock swell, knotting securely inside Carmen's tight, wet pussy. The sensation was unlike anything I'd ever experienced before, the primal intensity of our joining leaving me breathless.

"Fuck, yes," I growled through gritted teeth, holding her hips firmly to ensure our bond was complete.

At that moment, Axel let out a guttural roar, his release spurting across Carmen's hair and coating her dark strands with his hot semen. This only heightened the wild, feral atmosphere.

"Fuck, sorry, baby," Axel said, kissing her on the mouth.

"It's okay," she giggled, looking exhausted from pregnancy, and I knew we had pushed her to her limits as my cock swelled and knotted her to me.

"Our fiance about ready to sleep," Tyler remarked, rubbing her shoulders.

"I love you all," she mumbled, her voice barely more than a whisper, her eyelids barely open.

I reached out and tenderly touched her cheek, my fingers trembling slightly from the overwhelming emotions coursing through me.

"We love you too, Carmen," I murmured, feeling an inexplicable sense of protectiveness for the beautiful omega who had captured my heart. "More than you know."

As Carmen drifted into a well-deserved sleep between Tyler and me, I couldn't help but feel a fierce determination rising within me. I would do anything to keep her safe, to ensure her happiness. No one would ever take her away from me again—not as long as I was alive.

"Rest well, my love," I whispered into her ear, pressing a soft kiss to her temple. "We'll be here when you wake."

epilogue

. . .

Two Months Later

Carmen

"*S*top!" I cried, laughing as Griffin splashed water at me in the swimming pool. I was hanging out with all my alphas today on a hot summer day.

The sun's rays glistened on the surface of the water. I felt at peace with my pack—no tension and no worries. My laughter mingled with theirs until a sharp, intense cramp seized my body.

I cried out, clutching my belly as tears formed in my eyes from the contraction.

"Shit, Carmen, are you okay?" Tyler swam to my side, his hand protectively resting on my swollen stomach. His eyes searched mine, worry etched across his face.

"Ow!" I whimpered, squeezing my eyes shut against the pain. "It hurts so much."

But then the pain disappeared as quickly as it had come.

"Was that a contraction?" Logan asked, his eyes wide with instant alarm.

"Yes," I answered, scared of the next one.

"This might be it, guys," Griffin said. "Carmen, is it time to go to the hospital?"

I could only nod, unable to speak through the agony of the second contraction. An odd sensation engulfed me as I felt warmth spreading through the water around me. My heart raced—my water had broken.

"I think my water broke," I shouted as panic surged through me.

"Alright, let's get you to a hospital. Stay calm, honey," Jaxon said, lifting me out of the pool and carrying me toward the house to get dry.

I held onto the kitchen counter as Jaxon rushed upstairs to grab my hospital bag and clothes. My baby was coming today, I thought excitedly. I had been waiting forever, feeling tired and sluggish for months.

After a moment of reprieve, a third contraction took over my body, more powerful than the last one, and I screamed as Talon rubbed my lower back.

"Breathe, baby," he said. Jaxon rushed back downstairs with the huge hospital bag that I had spent days packing, along with a dry towel, while the rest of the pack hurried to put on dry clothes.

Jaxon and Talon worked quickly to help me remove my wet green bikini. I tried to assist, but another contraction hit, and I held onto Talon's shoulders as they quickly dressed me in a loose-flowing blue skirt and a black tank top.

"I'll have the van started!" shouted Axel urgently as I yelped from the pain.

Logan rushed into the kitchen after getting dressed and scooped me into his arms. "I got you, honey."

Moments later, I found myself in the front seat of the car, gripping the door handle as Axel drove us to the nearest hospital. My contractions grew stronger, leaving me screaming in pain. Fear threatened to choke me; this was my first time giving birth, and I didn't know what to expect.

"I'm never getting pregnant again!" I screamed through clenched teeth.

"We'll see about that," Griffin muttered from the backseat, a hint of amusement in his voice.

"Focus, Carmen. Breathe," Tyler instructed from behind me, his hand protectively resting on my stomach. But all I could think about was the pain and how scared I was.

THE STERILE SMELL of the hospital and the harsh fluorescent lights above did nothing to ease my fear as nurses rushed me inside.

"I need the pain meds," I groaned.

"We need to wait until you're dilated a bit more, or it can wear off during birth," the nurse said calmly.

Breathing hard, I sat on the birthing ball while holding onto the edge of the bed. I had no idea how I was going to continue to labor this way.

It was unbearable.

Tyler was right beside me, his scent calming me slightly as he coached me through each breath. "Take some deep breaths. I know you can do this. We all know how strong you are."

I gripped Logan's hand to my right tightly, my nails digging into his skin.

"It hurts so much," I sobbed, inhaling his citrus scent, which provided some comfort. Axel was purring into my neck, trying to relieve some of my pain. It helped, but it didn't change the fact that it felt like a chainsaw was ripping me apart below.

Talon and Griffin lingered nearby, trying not to crowd me but also keeping an eye out in case things went wrong.

"We can force them to give you pain relief," Tyler growled.

"No," I cried out.

After two hours of laboring and pain, the nurse returned to the room. "Alright, dear, let's see how far along you are."

I held back a scream as Tyler and Logan helped me onto the bed, laying me on my back. The nurse checked me and nodded.

"Am I ready?"

"Yes, you're dilated enough," she said with a smile. "I will let the team know, and they will administer the epidural."

I nodded quickly, eager for her to do just that. She left the room, and the alphas stood by in tense silence while Talon rubbed my back and Logan took over, purring as I lay on my side, moaning.

The anesthesiologist walked into the room, and the alphas cleared the bed to give him space.

"Are you ready for some pain relief?" he asked, and I nodded wordlessly through my pain. "You'll need to stay very still."

As he administered the medication, I could feel the effects slowly cascading through me. My lower body began to go numb, the intense pain fading away, leaving me feeling almost weightless.

"Thank God," I whispered, relief washing over me. The alphas visibly relaxed, sharing in my relief that the worst of the pain was over.

"That's for sure," said Axel, letting out a long breath. He looked visibly stressed after watching me in pain for hours, and I smiled, exhausted, as I lay on the bed.

"I need some shut-eye," I said, listening to our baby's strong heartbeat through the monitors as I closed my eyes.

"You'll need your strength," Tyler agreed, while Griffin kissed my forehead. I knew it was Griffin because of his beard, and I smiled again.

Hours later, the first light of dawn cast a soft glow on the sterile hospital room. Beads of sweat clung to my forehead, dampening my hair.

My body trembled with exhaustion as I gripped Tyler's and Logan's hands tightly, trying to muster the strength to push once more.

The pressure in my lower body was overwhelming, and I was losing strength.

"Here," said the nurse, offering me a sip of apple juice for energy. "This should help."

"Thanks," I mumbled, gratefully accepting the drink and feeling the sweet liquid reinvigorate me just enough.

"Alright, Carmen, you can do this. Push again," the doctor instructed firmly. My eyes clenched shut, and I groaned, feeling weak and battered.

"I can't," I whimpered, knowing that giving up wasn't an option.

Logan leaned in, looking deep into my eyes, his gaze filled with worry. I knew my alpha, and he was freaking out inside, even though he tried to hide it.

"You've been waiting to hold your baby," he said gruffly, emotion in his voice. "Push for the baby."

My heart raced, adrenaline pumping through my veins. Panting, I took a deep breath and pushed as hard as I could, willing myself to find the strength within me for my child.

"Come on, Carmen, just a little more," Tyler encouraged, squeezing my hand tighter, his eyes filled with worry and hope.

"Almost there!" the doctor called out, spurring me on despite the burning strain in my body.

The first cry of my newborn filled the air, a sound that pierced straight through to my soul. Tears streamed down my cheeks as I trembled with overwhelming joy and relief.

"It's a boy," the doctor announced. The alphas had big smiles on their faces.

"Oh my god," I choked out between sobs, my arms outstretched and eager. They placed him on my chest, skin-to-skin, as the baby's cries echoed in the small room. I spoke softly to him, my heart overwhelmed with love. "Oh goodness, Momma's got you now."

At the sound of my voice, he instantly calmed, his cries subsiding into tiny whimpers. I marveled at how such a small being could hold so much power over my heart, instantly bonding us together.

Talon leaned in, pressing a tender kiss to my forehead.

"You did such a good job, baby," he murmured proudly.

"Thank you," I whispered back, smiling through my exhaustion. I couldn't believe this perfect little life was finally here, in my arms.

Logan, Tyler, Griffin, Axel, and Jaxon gathered around us, their faces glowing with joy. Each took turns kissing me on the lips and admiring the baby.

"Look at what we've created," Logan said, his hand gently resting on my shoulder as he gazed at our son.

"He's beautiful," Talon agreed, emotion thick in his voice.

Griffin grinned, his eyes twinkling. "He's going to be one hell of an alpha someday."

Axel nodded, his usual stoic expression softened by love. "We'll make sure of it."

"Welcome to the family, little guy," Jaxon said. "Have we decided on a name?"

"We're leaving that to our omega," Logan replied, looking at me expectantly. "What's our son's name, honey?"

I smiled as I stroked his soft hair. "He looks like an Alaric."

"Alaric it is," Logan announced, and the alphas let out low growls of acceptance. "He is our firstborn son from the many children we will have."

"We have something for Carmen," Talon said, interrupting him. Logan looked surprised, and I scrunched my eyebrows in confusion as Talon presented a square box before me. "Open it."

While the baby rested on my chest, I smiled as I carefully lifted the lid of the box. I gasped when I saw a heavy, thick necklace made of gold and diamonds, shaped into a heart, along with matching earrings.

The alphas chuckled at my reaction, and I couldn't believe they had thought of this. I didn't care much about material things, but I was truly shocked.

"Your push gift, my love. You deserve it and more," Talon said. "The love of our pack."

THE END

You've reached the end of the *Howl's Edge: Omega for The Pack* series. Thank you for reading!

My next story will feature Lena (Carmen's sister) as she navigates the human life as a librarian hiding from her abusive alphas. This is her book: The Librarian and Her Alphas

thank you for reading!

Phew! You've made it to the end of the Howl's Edge Series. It was quite the journey, and I really hope you had a lot of fun reading through the series, as much as I enjoyed writing each and every book in the series.

Thank you so much for reading *Denied by The Alphas*. Check out my newest book, The Librarian and Her Alphas on Amazon.

I encourage you to join my mailing list so you can find out exactly when my next book release will be, and so you can stay up to date on any new audiobook releases as well.

Newsletter

For any questions, concerns, or inquiries, feel free to email me at author_laylasparks@yahoo.com

also by layla sparks

Howl's Edge Island: Omega For The Pack (COMPLETED Reverse Harem Series)

Book 1 (*Tiana's story*): Stolen by The Pack

Book 2 (*Keera's story*): Auctioned to the Pack

Book 3 (*Lyra's story*): Princess For The Pack

Book 4 (*Vanessa's story*): Betrayed by The Pack

Book 5 (*Jade's story*): Matched to The Pack

Book 6 (*Alana's story*): Knotted by The Pack

Book 7 (*Lacy's story*): Craved by The Pack

Book 8 (*Olivia's story*): Freed by The Pack

Dawn of The Alphas: Omega For The Pack Series

Book 1: Maid for The Alphas (*Breanna's story*)

Book 2: Promised to The Alphas (*Ruby's story*)

Book 3: Denied by The Alphas (*Carmen's story*)

The Librarian and Her Alphas (*Lena's story*)